A Forest of Gold

A Forest of Gold

Courtney Maika

Scholastic Canada Ltd.

Toronto New York London Auckland Sydney
Mexico City New Delhi Hong Kong Buenos Aires

Scholastic Canada Ltd.
604 King Street West, Toronto, Ontario M5V 1E1, Canada

Scholastic Inc.
557 Broadway, New York, NY 10012, USA

Scholastic Australia Pty Limited
PO Box 579, Gosford, NSW 2250, Australia

Scholastic New Zealand Limited
Private Bag 94407, Botany, Manukau 2163, New Zealand

Scholastic Children's Books
Euston House, 24 Eversholt Street, London NW1 1DB, UK

Cover images: iStockphoto.com/oversnap (silhouette),
iStockphoto.com/duncan1890 (banner)
Andrew Geiger/Getty Images (background)

Library and Archives Canada Cataloguing in Publication

Maika, Courtney, 1990-
A forest of gold / Courtney Maika.

ISBN 978-1-4431-0046-5

I. Title.

PS8626.A417435F67 2011   jC813'.6   C2011-901857-8

6 5 4 3 2 1   Printed in Canada 121   11 12 13 14 15

MIX
Paper from
responsible sources
FSC® C004071

For my mom, Donna, who was my first editor, and also to Dad and Brittany. To Grandma and Grandpa Novack too, who helped me with research and inspired events without realizing it. I thank God for His gifts.

FRIDAY, SEPTEMBER 9, 1927

Happy twelfth birthday to me! I am so excited! Mr. Roberts just stopped by to drop off the Singer sewing machine Mrs. Roberts had borrowed from Mother until Mrs. Roberts' new one comes in, and he said he had a surprise for my birthday. I had been in the kitchen with Mother and Mary, trying to keep Alex from sticking his fingers in my birthday cake batter, when Pa called me to the door. Mr. Roberts wished me a Happy Birthday and said he had a gift for me from William and that he thought Mother might let me open it, despite her present need of my baking skills. After saying this, he glanced up at Mother, who had also come to the door, and she told me to go ahead and open it.

I did and when I saw that it was a journal I begged Mother to let me come up to my room and write in it. She told me to run up but not to spend too long. I promised her that I wouldn't. I can *hardly* contain my excitement.

There. I just got up and did a little dance around my room. I feel that that is not a good enough expression of my happiness, so I think that after supper and chores, I will go down to the store and thank Will personally. I have to go now, because Mother is calling me. How can she, when she knows that I have just begun writing in my first-ever journal? I won't ask her that because I would be scolded for being impertinent and then she would say, "Time waits for no man, Emily."

I have decided to use this journal as a place where I can be "the voice of history." Mr. Meredith, the postmaster, loves history. To him, everything is either "the voice of history" or "history in the making." I suppose he's right. I know that whenever Mother tells me a story about people I've never known, like my Mémère Bilodeau, I think of how much I wish I knew more about them. If only those people had left behind a journal like I'm writing in now! So if I fill this book with all of the things that happen to me, full of our family stories, maybe my daughters or granddaughters or nieces can read it and know all about us Pattersens and our antics.

I opened the rest of my birthday gifts after supper.

From Mother and Pa I got a beautiful new store-bought dress! It is navy blue and has a wide white collar and it falls just below my knees. I tried it on and Joe said I looked very spiffy. Pa said it reminded him of the dress I was wearing when I met the Prince.

Alex didn't know the story, so of course Pa said that he was talking about the second of September, 1919, when the Prince of Wales visited North Bay. I was only three years old (almost four), Joe was seven, Alex was just a baby, and Mother and Pa and Uncle Mathieu and Pépère took us up to North Bay to see the Prince. When I saw him I started yelling and laughing and waving and jumping up and down and the Prince smiled and waved at me. It's true that I was wearing a blue dress, but I hope I have changed in other ways since then!

From Joe I got a book called *Anne of Green Gables*, by Lucy Maud Montgomery, which I have heard about and am excited to read. Alex gave me a very nice paper he wrote himself and it is titled "How to Win A Snowball Fight (Since You Are Not A Boy)" — only he spelled "since" (and some other words) wrong. He is excited for winter. I will paste the paper in here as a keepsake.

HOW TO WIN A SNOWBALL FIGHT
(SINSE YOU ARE NOT A BOY)

1. make sure the snow is stiky
2. gather some snow in your hands
3. press it together and turn it over in your hands till it is in the shape of a ball
4. throw it reelly hard at someone but not your brothers
5. keep doing this till you win but make shur you don't get hit by anyone elses snowballs

Of course I'm always sure to do these things, except I *do* aim the snowballs at my brothers!

The aunts and uncles bought me a little clock. Auntie Annabelle picked it out and the Relatives in England sent a card saying that it is from them, too. It is a nice little size and I have it on the night table beside my bed. Mother said it will be perfect for my fireplace mantel when I get married! I asked how she could be so sure that I am going to get married at all, and she grinned and said that that's how she used to think until she met Pa!

That got me thinking about Pa and his past and about how proud I am to have a father who is determined and knows how to make do. He runs the farm, and he does very well for having come from England on his own as a young man with almost no experience in farming. He says that what he did know he learned from spending his boyhood summers helping on his uncle's farm in the country.

Pépère Bilodeau gave the farm to Pa when he died, instead of to Uncle Mathieu. It was supposed to go to Uncle Mathieu, except he had already inherited his father-in-law's business as a butcher. So since our family had already been living on this farm to take care of Pépère, it went to Mother and Pa. I've heard people say that Pa came into Old Money by marrying Mother. Pa says we are blessed to be more or less in the middle class because farming isn't usually the most secure thing. It depends so much on nature. Even as it is, Pa spends the winters working in the lumber camps because our farm doesn't bring in money in the cold seasons.

P.S. I didn't get to thank Will for the journal. Maybe tomorrow.

SATURDAY, SEPTEMBER 10, 1927

I've finished my morning chores and I don't have to do the breakfast dishes because it is Saturday and Mary is here to do them. I must say that I was a little bad-tempered about my chores this morning and I made the mistake of grumbling in front of Mary about how Mother makes me do so many chores. I know one or two girls at school who have to do hardly *anything* around their houses. That got Mary on her big speech about how my mother is a complete lady and that if Mother thinks it's important for her only daughter to do Saturday chores, then it must be important indeed.

But I *also* know how important Mother thinks it is for girls to receive an education and "thereby better themselves." In front of Mary, though, Mother plays the role of the sweet-tempered housewife perfectly. One day I asked Mother why she is so graceful and sweeping around Mary. She told me that when Mary was my age her pa made her quit school because her family needed her to work to help bring in money, and that Mary didn't want to quit. I don't know what I would do if I had to quit school to help on the farm. Mother said she has a Duty to be the best example that she can be for Mary.

Mother says everyone is put on God's Good Earth for a reason and I think Mother's is to let everyone know about Duty. She loves making the most boring tasks into Duties — she says they build Character.

———————————

Just a minute ago Joe stopped by my room on his way downstairs. I was sitting at my desk writing out my spelling words for practice and he asked me why on earth I was doing homework on a Saturday. I reminded him that I hope to be a teacher. He doesn't quite understand why anyone would want to do that, I think. Joe was good at school, but he never liked it as much as I do.

He has confided in me that he dreams of leaving town and becoming a very rich entrepreneur through some endeavour such as the lumber industry, just like J. R. Booth did with the square timber trade and the railway. But for starts he wants to work in a lumber camp this winter. Last time Joe said this to me, I told him that the idea of his leaving made me sad, and besides, he could become just as rich or richer if he were to be something like a lawyer. I told him he should go to college instead of looking for adventure Who Knows Where. He just sighed and said, "Yes, Em, that is what *you* think, because you are going to become a teacher, and live to be one of the wisest grannies in this town. I already pity the poor children who will have to sit through your lectures." I laughed in spite of myself and chased him outside. Mary, who was peeling potatoes on the porch, told me to act like a lady and not to chase my brothers all over the house. "At least she's chasing her brothers, and not the boys from school," Joe sang. Then he ran off, most likely to Roberts' store. He likes to go there as an escape from our place, and none of the Robertses mind because when he's there he helps load customers' wagons and everything.

I think he gets most of his extravagant ideas from Andrew Roberts, who knows anything and everything to do with impressive places to travel. Even though Andrew is a couple of years older than Joe, they get along fine. Andrew has worked in the lumber camps for a few years now, and he's planning on returning this year. Joe looks up to Andrew, and is very jealous when he leaves for the camps in the fall. Every year Pa tells Joe that he can join Pa in the camps once he's learned not to turn so hot-headed in an instant. He says the camps are dangerous enough without Tempers added into the mix. When Pa says this Joe always stomps out of the house and slams the door.

I must say that I would not be too eager to let Joe go to the camps either, if his temper would cause him problems. Just yesterday he bruised the knuckles on both of his hands by punching the kitchen door frame, all because Pa wouldn't let him make a dinner-hour delivery to the Rosemount side of town with Andrew! He was happy enough the next minute, but it's these outbursts that Pa says worry him.

Once, I asked Joe why he lets such small things anger him but he was annoyed with me so he only answered, "Reasons." I wish I could use Reasons as an excuse. I can imagine how that would please Mother. "Emily Marie Pattersen! Why aren't the floors swept and the pigs fed and the eggs collected and the cows milked?" And I could just say, "Reasons!"

I have to go. Mother is calling, and if I don't show up soon, she's sure to assign me a Duty.

Mother was looking for the pot that we use for making stew because it wasn't where it belongs. I found it in a corner of Alex and Joe's room (on Alex's side, of course) and it had a pair of trousers, five sticks, two rocks and a couple of handfuls of sand in it. *I* had to wash it out but then Mother let me go to the store to thank Will for this journal.

I guess William is my best friend, especially since Amelia moved to Ottawa three years ago after her father went there looking for a better job. Her mother was anxious to leave Mattawa anyway because she grew up in Montréal and wanted a city life again. I miss Amelia sometimes, especially when Will is off doing something with the boys. She does write to me, but not often. Her letters make her sound as though her nose may be in the air now, though. Maybe it's because she's at a private school, or maybe she thinks she's better than people who live in small towns.

Anyhow, I finally got to thank Will for giving me this book. I looked for him at the store first but he wasn't there, so I went to the place where he was next most likely to be: the train station. He loves following the station master around, and Mr. Rankin is the kind of person who loves to show "young'uns" how to do things. He always calls Will "Mr. Roberts" or "young sir," as though they were business partners. Mr. Rankin and Will are like the best of friends, if you leave out the fact that Mr. Rankin is in his fifties.

I found Will at the station, and can you believe what he said when I thanked him for this book? He told me that he hopes I write about the people around me be-cause he has arranged for Joe to sneak this journal to him when it's full so he knows what I really think about him! It made me blush — it is *so* easy to make me blush, and it seems that everyone takes advantage of it! I hope he was joking. I think he was, but of course I can't be sure. I'll have to find a hiding place for this book!

I'm going to read more of *Anne of Green Gables* now.

I finished writing a letter to Amelia today, and when I signed my name I got thinking about how glad I am that Pa insisted on spelling my first name the English way, instead of the French *Emilie*. I think *Emilie* looks too much like *Emile*, which is a boy's name. Mother said that if my first and last names both had to be English, she would make sure my middle name was French, and I am glad it is, otherwise it would look and sound so plain.

Bedtime for me!

SUNDAY, SEPTEMBER 11, 1927

Church today. Father Duquette has been the priest here at Ste. Anne's for as long as I can remember. Mother says it has been ten years now, so I was only about two when he came. She says that before him was Father Paquette, the priest who married Mother and Pa. (He didn't actually get married TO them, of course.)

This may be a very un-Christian thing to say, but it is the truth and at least I am writing it down instead of gossiping about it.

Mary is wearing on my nerves! She isn't working

here today but she "stopped in to see how things are" after church. I know that is not the whole truth. She only comes by because she is sweet on Andrew Roberts and hopes his family will be here visiting when she is. Visiting our house is more appropriate than calling at the Robertses' because she doesn't know them very well. I am so sure she is sweet on Andrew because the last time she came for a Sunday visit when Andrew was here, she wouldn't stop looking at him and she giggled at EVERYTHING he said, even if it was absolutely not funny. For example:

Andrew (on a cloudy, rainy, blustery day): "This rain'll be good for your crops, Mr. Pattersen."

Mary: giggle, giggle, GIGGLE.

I often grow tired of Mary's chattering, but Mother tells me to treat my enduring it as a Duty that will help build Character in me. I consider it more of a Burden than a Duty. Pa, on the other hand, will send me to the barn to do some chore or other if he sees that my ears are being talked off. Once he asked me to tidy up some nails and wood scraps that had been left on the floor of the loft. "Some things may have been *shuffled* around, Em, and I want everything in its place for tomorrow morning." He emphasized the word "shuffled" but Mary didn't notice. I went into the barn and saw that nothing was out of place, but there was a game of Beat the Devil unfinished on the loft floor, so I finished it for Pa. (I won!) Pa has an odd habit of keeping a deck of cards in the barn in case he ever needs to "calm his mind." Mother suspects that it causes him to waste time, but I know that he only plays Beat the Devil out there when he needs to get away from the house.

When I came back to the kitchen after finishing the game, Pa asked me if everything was tidy. I just grinned, and before Mary could start talking to me again, Pa and I started singing "The Jolly Raftsman O."

> To hew and score it is his plan,
> And handle the broad-axe neatly O.
> It's lay the line and mark the pine
> And do it most completely O.

School tomorrow. This will only be the second week, so I am not tired of it. I think I will read a little more of my book before bed. I wish the characters were real. I would like to say I'm like Anne, but really I'm probably more like Jane Andrews. High-class Miss Tilly Boulanger is Josie Pye through and through. Will and Joe are both like Gilbert or Moody, with their constant teasing, and Mother is most definitely a Marilla!

MONDAY, SEPTEMBER 12, 1927

Quite a bit of excitement at school today! Clarence Prince got in trouble and Tilly and Jason Boulanger aren't speaking to him! I didn't see all of what happened — I only heard a commotion and saw Tilly run from the room holding a handkerchief to her arm — but Will and Alex explained it to me before I went to the girls' side of the yard at dinner. Alex didn't see what happened either, because he is in the class of younger students, but he still made dramatic interjections while Will was telling the story. It happened during dictation (which was an exception because we usually have dictations on Friday, but last week Sister Agatha said we could have it this Monday "as a treat" for doing so well in the first week of school).

Anyhow, Clarence caught Tilly sneaking peeks at his paper and he got so angry he jabbed his pen right into her arm! (Alex interjection: He JABBED it, Em!) Tilly yelled (SCREAMED!), which of course I heard, and jerked her arm away. (The pen came out with a SQUELCH, Em!) Clarence looked sorry right away, and when he offered Tilly his hanky, she grabbed (SNATCHED!) it from him and ran (SKEDADDLED) from the room.

I saw the rest. Clarence got the strap and even though he apologized, Tilly and her brother won't talk to him. I guess I wouldn't talk to someone who had just stabbed me with a pen, but then again, I would never cheat. Have to go help with supper.

TUESDAY, SEPTEMBER 13, 1927

Neither Tilly nor Clarence was at school today. I suppose Tilly's arm is too sore to write and if Will is a true judge of Clarence's pa, Clarence's bottom is too sore to sit on.

Wednesday, September 14, 1927

Today was boring. Boring, boring, boring. There must be something I can write that isn't boring. No one got the strap today, no one had to stand in the corner, and Sister Agatha didn't yell at anyone. Not that I *want* those things to happen, of course! Both Tilly and Clarence were back, and Tilly and Jason seem to be talking to Clarence again.

Thursday, September 15, 1927

Today on the way home, me, Alex, Will and some of the others from school went down to the shores of the Mattawa River to search for arrowheads. Pépère Bilodeau used to tell us that in the old days it was commonplace for people to find arrowheads and other things along the Mattawa. He said you can be sure that anything you find was left behind by the Indian tribes that used to live here. Sister Agatha told us that the Indians were here long before Étienne Brûlé even thought about coming along in his canoe to explore. Some of the tools are even thousands of years old! Alex has always wanted to find an arrowhead and he's spent many hours searching. Today he was finally lucky.

We were all looking among the rocks and sand when we heard Alex yell, "I found one! Over here!" so we all ran and he *had* found one and Pa says it is made of BONE! It was quite large, too, not one of those boring small ones. Then, not far away I found what Pa says is the stem of a clay pipe. It is very exciting to have. I cleaned it and placed it in my old hanky in my dresser drawer with all of my other special things. I like to wonder where the barrel of the pipe is. Is it lying a few feet away from the place that I found the stem, under a bit of sand? Or has it been carried away to Ottawa, or to the St. Lawrence River? Is it clay again, broken into millions of little pieces that make up the river bottoms?

———————————

I cannot believe it. Will, being the oh-so-wonderful friend that he is, has just stopped by to tell me that he gets to go to North Bay tomorrow for Children's Day at the fair. He will miss the entire day of school! I begged Mother to allow me and Alex to go. Of course she said no. I know we can afford it, but Mother doesn't believe in taking us out of school unless there is a Serious Reason (which is if someone dies, or we are so sick that we can't stay still for a minute without getting up to use the you-know-what). In my opinion, the fair in North Bay is a Serious Reason, but Mother doesn't see it that way.

It is not Christian to envy others but neither is it Christian to lie, so I will tell the truth — I am envious of Will.

FRIDAY, SEPTEMBER 16, 1927

I have the most EXCITING NEWS! We went to North Bay this afternoon, for Children's Day! Pa must have convinced Mother to let us go because they were waiting for us in the schoolyard at dinnertime. Pa told Sister Mary of the Cross that Alex and me would be absent for the afternoon.

Sister looked disapproving, but I didn't care and couldn't hide my smiles as we rushed off to the train.

The fair was wonderful — they had a new carousel this year, and I went on it plenty of times, although I felt a little old for it. We looked at all of the animals and Pa said that if we lived closer he would enter Whinny and Wilfrid in the show for workhorses.

Will found us and he took us to buy candied apples and toffee and other goodies. He had already eaten *two* candied apples, and he bought his third with us. His pa gave him a whole fifty-cent piece to spend! Alex and I each got a quarter. The colours and the people and the rides and the laughter were wonderful, but I must say that I'm happy to be off to bed now!

SATURDAY, SEPTEMBER 17, 1927

I am snatching a little bit of time to write before I go down for breakfast. I know that, because it's harvest time, Saturdays will be fuller of chores than usual. I am looking forward to winter when all this bustling about the farm will be over and everyone and everything will be settled cozily in for the winter. Today I will have to help with breakfast, which is usual, and I will also have to do the dishes, which is unusual for a Saturday. Then Mother, Mary and I will be doing all sorts of kitcheny things because the Wilsons are threshing this weekend and Mother is bringing them some doughnuts and cookies, which have yet to be made!

Mother is calling.

Sunday, September 18, 1927

Alex made up a poem on the way home from church today. Here it is.

Cows Eat Grass

By Alexander John Adelard Pattersen

Cows eat grass.
Cows eat grass.
We're on our way to Mass, and the Cows eat
     grass.
The same field we pass
On our way BACK from Mass
And still, Still, STILL,
The Cows eat grass.

Cleverly titled. Pa and Joe and I laughed when Alex recited it and Mother said it was sacrilegious, but I'm sure she found it funny because she kept calling him her little poet. I told Alex I like it and he wondered aloud about whether he should recite it for Father Duquette next weekend. I told him honestly that I didn't think Mother would approve of that, but that he should recite it for Will on Monday. The fact that I thought it was good enough to recite for Will seemed to hearten him, and he absolutely beamed when I told him I would write it in here. He wanted his full name written, which surprised me because he has been embarrassed about it ever since Joe teased him that with a name like that he is destined to become Prime Minister. He told me to write "back" in "big" letters to "empathize" the word.

(He meant emphasize.) "It's so that people will know that the cows have been there for a REALLY long time, Em," he explained matter-of-factly. He was also concerned about form and he watched me write it to make sure I did everything properly.

Everyone has gone to bed early tonight because Pa and Joe are going to start cutting the grain tomorrow.

Monday, September 19, 1927

Alex recited "Cows Eat Grass" for Will on the way to school this morning and Will laughed over it for a long time. Alex was as pleased as punch.

After school I had to go out to the field and help stook grain while Mother cooked supper. At least it is done now. Stooking grain is pretty tiring and the freshly cut stalks are so sharp and scratchy that they make my legs itch. And it's annoying when all the bugs get stirred up and land all over me or fly in my eyes and mouth. Bugs hate grain-cutting time because it leaves them with no place to hide. At least there aren't many mosquitoes at this time of year. And the freshly cut grain does smell lovely! I think next time I stook I will borrow a pair of Joe's pants, even if I have to tie them with cord at the waist to keep them up.

This year Pa let Joe drive Whinny and Wilfrid, who pulled the binder. Pa always calls the binder Master Massey because it was made by the Massey-Harris machine company. Master Massey cut and bundled the grain, and Pa, Alex and I followed behind. I had to remind Alex to stand the bundles together in pairs, like an upside-down V, because every year he seems to think heaping them in piles is good enough. If Alex were in charge of stooking, the grain would never dry.

We had only got about fifteen minutes in when the Master ran out of twine, so *I* had to run into town to get some more. Pa figured that by the time he got Whinny and Wilfrid unhitched I could be halfway to town and back, if I ran "like the wind." I did run like the wind and I was in need of some when I got back. Joe told us that he had noticed that the binder needed more twine when he was getting it ready last Wednesday, but then I had come in to ask him about something and he forgot. I'm going to bed now.

P.S. Speaking of going to bed — something I will not complain about when it comes to cutting the grain is the fresh straw. As soon as Mr. McConnell comes around with the threshing mill, we can refill our ticks! I remember when I was little I asked Pa why we thrash the grain if it hadn't done anything wrong, and I was embarrassed when he told me that we pronounce it *threshing* and that all it does is separate the grain from the stalk, so that we're left with oats and straw.

TUESDAY, SEPTEMBER 20, 1927
You will never guess what Tilly did today! We were in the cloakroom, taking off our coats, when she said in a very condescending voice, "Emily, you have a piece of *straw* on your coat. Won't you remove it and throw it into

the stove before it catches on my *new* dress? Honestly, farmers have no sense of cleanliness."

I was very rude back. I said, "Tilly, you make such *sour* comments. Won't you remove them and throw them into the stove before they infect your perfectly *angelic* disposition? Honestly, you hardly know how to flatter yourself." I felt *kind* of bad then, and she looked positively furious. Her friend Marilyn called to her at that moment, so I was saved from having to hear a retort, and she was saved from having to think of one!

On a Tilly-free note, I have been bringing *Anne of Green Gables* to school to read at dinnertime and I finished it for the second time today. It is one of the loveliest books I have ever read. Anne is a true heroine and I am glad that things work out for her. Sometimes I wish I were an interesting heroine rather than just Emily Pattersen. But whenever I say something like that out loud, Pa quotes one of his favourite Bible verses: "'For I know the plans I have for you,' says the Lord . . . " Like Mother, Pa believes that everyone is here on Earth for a specific reason. I like that thought.

WEDNESDAY, SEPTEMBER 21, 1927

It seems that everyone around me is busy, busy, busy getting ready for winter. Even though the grain is all cut I am kept from playing after school by digging potatoes and pickling. The potato digging goes slower than it should because Alex is too young to do it yet. Pa let him try but he kept slicing the potatoes open with the hoe.

So it is his job to put the potatoes into buckets and carry them to the cellar and dump them into the wooden bins in the corner. But this goes slowly too because Alex can't carry more than one bucket at once.

And pickling and canning is no ride on the hay wagon either. (How is that for a saying? Mr. Meredith uses sayings all the time so I decided to try my own.) Wash, slice. Wash, slice. Wash, slice. Wash, slice. Imagine me filling up the rest of this journal with those two words repeated over and over. And imagine having to read EVERY single one of those words. That is how boring pickling is. I could say that I am thankful for the pickled cucumbers and beets and everything in the winter, but that would take the effect away from my complaining.

Besides all of the farm work, town is getting busier and the hotels are filling up with men who have come looking for winter work in a lumber operation. It seems as though EVERYONE is talking about the lumber season and whether they will cut privately or work in a camp this year, and who the best jobbers are, and how much money they hope to make and on and On and ON. Pa still shows no sign of letting Joe go with him to a lumber camp this year, but Joe acts like he's going anyway.

I feel sorry for Joe. I wish he could go just so he'd be happy. I wonder if I should ask Pa why he doesn't let Joe go with him, or if that would be interfering. I have to go to bed now. I'm pretty tired!

P.S. Maybe my ride-on-the-hay-wagon saying is not so good — hay wagon rides are bumpy.

Thursday, September 22, 1927

I almost wish that no one liked pickled goods so that we wouldn't have to make them.

I stopped by the store on the way home from school today and Will let Alex and me each try a piece of the new penny candy his father got in a few days ago. I was excited at first because it was so colourful, but it just tasted like mint. I like mint, but I had been expecting something more exciting to match the colours. Sometimes I wish Pa owned a store. Then we would be rich and not have to stook grain and pickle cucumbers and dig potatoes and milk cows and gather eggs and feed horses. And muck out barns. But on the other hand, I love our animals and at least we are not so poor that we can't afford to hire extra help now and then.

Friday, September 23, 1927

I've finally found a permanent hiding place for this journal in my room. At first I had it in my dresser drawer with the rosary I got for my First Communion, along with my other special things. But I was afraid that that was too obvious a place, so now I am keeping it on a little ledge just inside the underside of my bed, so I can get it by crouching down and reaching for it. I have to admit that I wouldn't be surprised if Alex somehow found it there, but I am willing to take that chance because I can think of no better place unless the place isn't in my room. And I'm not willing to trudge to places like the barn or the cellar in forty below or at midnight when I want to write!

I am somewhat suspicious of Joe right now, although maybe I have no reason to be, since he and Andrew have been scheming at different things all their lives. Today I stopped in at the store on the way home from school and Mr. Roberts asked me if I wanted to bring him a new roll of packing twine from the storeroom! Maybe it doesn't sound all that exciting, but the storeroom is one place where Will's friends aren't usually allowed, so it was a treat for me to go back there. And when I opened the door, who did I find but Joe and Andrew, talking quietly! I only heard Andrew say, "your uncle," as I opened the door, because they stopped talking as soon as they saw me. They pretended that they had been moving some heavy boxes around and I pretended I hadn't known they were talking. I didn't ask what they were up to because I didn't want to seem like a little pest and they would never have told me anyway. "Your uncle . . . " What about our uncle? Which uncle did Andrew mean? Uncle Mathieu, or Uncle Timothy?

SATURDAY, SEPTEMBER 24, 1927

Today was so much fun. After breakfast I decided to go for a walk to the store to buy some more writing paper for my next letter to Amelia. Will was there so I asked him if he wanted to come for a walk. He asked where I was going and I said nowhere so he said he'd better come and make sure I didn't waste my time going nowhere and spent it usefully going somewhere. I knew that he had something in mind, especially when he went around the back of the store to get his wagon. When we stopped at Clarence's house to ask if he wanted to join us, I knew I was about to witness some mischief. Will's mother says that Will and Clarence are a recipe for trouble, but I say they are a recipe for fun. It often seems that an adult's Trouble is a child's Fun.

We crossed the bridge to the Rosemount side of town and went up to the hilly streets and that's when Will told us his idea was to ride down the street in the wagon! I tried to convince the boys not to do it because it was dangerous but they said not to be such a sissy. "Sticks and stones!" I said. I stood there for a while with my arms folded, watching them and trying to look stern. I couldn't do it for long. "Fine," I said. "I'll try once." I was quite sure I would go more than once but of course I didn't say that.

I went and it was so, SO fun! It was a little scary at first because Will gave me a big running push and it felt like I would never stop and I was going to roll right into the river. But of course the river was farther than it seemed and I stopped being nervous. We went again and again and some others came out with their wagons to join us and we had races. I think we were there for about two hours until I said I had to go home to do chores. I didn't want to leave, but I knew I had to help bring the grain to the barn to get it ready for threshing. Mr. McConnell is coming with the threshing machine early Monday morning, and we can't bring in any grain tomorrow because it is Sunday. We'll have to have wagon races again sometime.

Sunday, September 25, 1927

No wagon races today. We went to church and the Robertses came visiting after. It was nice, but not as fun as flying down a hill in a wagon. I showed Will how much I have written in this journal, but I made sure he didn't see me take it from its hiding place. He seemed pleased that I have already written so much.

We are VERY lucky that it didn't rain this week, and that we could leave the grain out to dry for such a long time. I'll be glad when the threshing is done because it will be one less thing making everyone busy. I am thankful that I'm allowed to go to school every day during the fall harvest. Almost none of the older boys has been in class these past few days and many of the girls are kept home to help as well. I suppose it might be nice to stay home tomorrow, because it is fun to visit with everyone who comes to help with the threshing. On the other hand, I will not miss spending the day in the kitchen, helping Mother and who-knows-how-many other ladies cook for the men.

Monday, September 26, 1927

The apples will be ready for picking soon. We just need a few more light frosts to sweeten them up a bit, even though it's difficult to sweeten crabapples using anything but sugar. Then we will be making applesauce as much as we had been pickling.

AND, the best part of today is that the grain has been threshed and we have new, fresh, wonderful straw to fill our ticks! Mother sewed new ticks for us on her Singer, using the flour bags she's been saving, so it's like getting a whole new bed! (Except that my bed creaks.) I love the soft fluffiness of the new tick, and the sweet scent of the fresh straw. It reminds me of the barn (without the manure). My old tick was flat and it was beginning to smell musty, despite all of the airings and re-fluffings over the summer.

WEDNESDAY, SEPTEMBER 28, 1927

Even though we have a smaller class than usual, we had a Spelling Bee at school today to prepare us for Friday's test. I came in second. Tilly won. I would like to say that she cheated, but that wouldn't be very Christian of me when I have no evidence of it. The word I lost on was *impertinence*. I know how to spell it now! I spelled it i-m-p-e-r-t-i-n-I-n-c-e, with an *i* where there should have been an *e*. Oh well. Pa says to learn from our mistakes and I will. I'll get a perfect score on Friday's test.

FRIDAY, SEPTEMBER 30, 1927

I wish we didn't always have Spelling tests after Mental Arithmetic, because Mental Arithmetic makes my brain feel worn out. But I still got a perfect score on today's Spelling test! Sister A. handed them back in the afternoon. Tilly tried to find out my score but I wouldn't tell her. I think I almost drove her mad.

T.B.: How did you find the Spelling test, Emily?

E.P.: Fine.

T.B.: You must have studied hard.

E.P.: Yes, I did.

T.B.: You probably did better than me.

E.P.: Maybe. My mother says that what happens happens, and there's nothing I can do about it, so I don't trouble myself.

Then Will and Alex appeared and we came home.

SATURDAY, OCTOBER 1, 1927

It's pouring rain. We are very lucky to have all of our oats and straw cozy and dry in the barn. I think I will start a new book today.

MONDAY, OCTOBER 3, 1927

In a week it will be Joe's birthday! I have to start thinking of what I can give him. Maybe an idea will come to me while I help put away the wash.

TUESDAY, OCTOBER 4, 1927

I don't know if I will be able to sleep another wink in my life until I get to the bottom of what I am going to call the Lumber Camp Mystery. (L.C.M. for short.) Today I think I got more of a clue about why Pa is so set on Joe not going to the camps, except I can't figure out what it means.

Alex went with one of his friends to check for mail at the post office after school today and I went to the store with Will to get Alex a new pencil, because he snapped his. (Don't ask me how.) Mr. Roberts was busy in the storeroom, so Will looked for the pencils. While he was fiddling around behind the counter looking for the box, I saw a sign advertising Roberts' as the place to purchase warm clothing for the lumber camps. This reminded me of Joe and Pa, so I told Will the whole story about how Joe wants to go to the bush but Pa won't let him.

While I was telling Will the story, I noticed that gossipy old Miss Adams — that may be un-Christian to say but it is true — was paying very close attention. She had been hovering around the sugar for an unreasonably long time. She must have known that I knew she was listening because when I looked at her she assumed a very knowing look and said, "Well, Deary, maybe your brother has some growing up to do. Besides, after what happened to your uncle on the river, it's no wonder your Pa wants to keep his son away until he's wisened up a bit. I'll take two pounds of sugar, William, my boy."

Will rang up the sugar and when Miss Adams left we discussed the possible meanings of what Miss A. had said. What happened to Uncle Mathieu? He seems fine to me, and Miss A. can't be talking about Uncle Timothy, because he never worked in a camp and he's not from here anyway. Knowing how Uncle Mathieu likes to tell stories, it's a wonder he hasn't told us this one. It must be very private for him not to have said anything before. I wonder if I should ask about it? Probably not, in case I cause more trouble than it's worth.

THURSDAY, OCTOBER 6, 1927

There is some excitement at our house — Mother has had a letter from Auntie Mai in Pembroke. She read it out to us after supper and it says that Auntie Mai will be coming for a visit sometime early in November. She didn't give us an exact date and she says that she can walk herself from the station to our house. So we will have no notice of her arrival! In her letter Auntie Mai said that she misses her Dear Sister, and besides, "what better time of year to have a visit than in the dead of autumn when the leaves have fallen and sadness is waiting to seep into one's soul?"

Joe snickered when Mother got to this part. Mother shot Joe a Look but didn't say anything. If I had snickered I would have been given a Duty.

Auntie Mai also mentioned that her children wear on her nerves around this time of year, when mornings are spent trying to wrestle them into long underwear (I secretly laughed at this bit too) and school projects are being handed out and the like. Then, in the very next sentence she said that during the day it gets so quiet she can hardly stand it. Apparently, she will leave the children with a retired schoolteacher from down their street so that Uncle Timothy can be left on his own to work in peace.

The whole thing sounds suspicious to me — like she

is trying to get away from her own children. I mentioned this to Joe later on when we were upstairs and Mother and Pa were in the kitchen. Joe said that she *is* trying to get away from her own children. I asked what he meant and he said that he remembers them from when he was little, before Auntie and Uncle moved to Pembroke. He says that they are spoiled and conceited and that Auntie doesn't know how to control them. I feel sorry for the poor old schoolteacher who will be looking after them.

SATURDAY, OCTOBER 8, 1927

Lots of applesauce making this weekend.

I haven't made a decision about what to give Joe for his birthday, but I'll think some more about it while Alex and I milk Bess and Walter. (What possessed Alex to give a boy's name to a cow? I think his five-year-old heart was set on it!)

The more I pay attention, the more I realize why Pa doesn't want to let Joe go to a lumber camp with him. Not only is he hot-tempered, he can also be a daredevil when his friends put him up to it. Pa drove me to the store after supper today so I could buy Joe's birthday gift. I paid for my things and Mr. Roberts suggested I go look for Will in the backyard while he and Pa talked about seed for the spring crops.

So I went around to the back of the house and found Will crouched behind their big old maple. He saw me and motioned for me to be quiet and join him. I did and he said, "Look at them! This is going to be the perfect thing for me to hold over Andrew's head!" I gulped and peeked out from behind the tree. There was Joe, standing on the roof of the Robertses' shed, about to jump into a pile of leaves that was far too small to break his fall! Andrew and two older boys were watching. One jeered at him, "Aw, come on, Pattersen, be a man!" Joe hardly hesitated after that. He jumped. I managed not to yell, and then Will jerked me back behind the tree before I'd decided what to do next. "Don't you dare let Andrew know that we saw, or he'll get me good!" Will said. Just then I heard Pa call me from the front. "Fine," I agreed. I took one last glance at Joe and I flitted back to find Pa. None of the older boys saw me because they were all crowded around Joe, who was standing up. He seemed to have hurt his hand. I haven't seen him since, so I don't know how bad he's hurt.

MONDAY, OCTOBER 10, 1927

It is Joe's sixteenth birthday today! I'm up early this morning because I know that this evening I'll be busy helping Mother in the kitchen. Mary isn't coming to help because she's needed at her own house. Uncle Mathieu and Auntie Annabelle are coming over for supper.

I haven't mentioned what I bought for Joe. It is three peppermints and a handkerchief. I made the handkerchief out of a scrap of cloth that Mr. Roberts gave me for free. I know the handkerchief isn't very exciting but

I've embroidered Joe's initials — *JHP* for Joseph Hilaire Pattersen — in one corner. I've put the mints inside of it and wrapped it that way.

P.S. Joe's wrist appears to be sprained, but he hides it quite well. Alex told me he heard Joe telling Pa that he hurt it falling off the loft ladder and that Pa said, "Oh really?" as if he didn't believe him at all. I wonder if he saw anything Saturday night at the store, or if he suspects something but just doesn't know the specifics.

———————————

Joe liked my gift! He said my idea to wrap the peppermints in the handkerchief was nifty. He also got a new pocket knife from Mother and Pa, and Alex made him a slingshot. And Mother baked a cake, of course, to go with all of the other things we had prepared! Pa butchered one of our chickens for supper. It was SO good, and there are plenty of leftovers! Everyone was in a good mood and Uncle Mathieu even taught Alex some card tricks.

TUESDAY, OCTOBER 11, 1927
Alex is making us all crazy with his card tricks! He shows them to anyone and everyone. Sister Bridget had to take the deck from him at school, but she made the mistake of giving them back to him at dismissal, on the condition that he would never bring them to school again. She said cards are vulgar and "instruments of the devil." I wish she had given them back on

the condition that he would never annoy people with them again.

WEDNESDAY, OCTOBER 12, 1927

I am so angry right now — life is so unfair! I really needed to use the outhouse when I got home from school but Alex got to it first. So I was patient and came into the house to set down my dinner pail and books and change out of my school clothes. I went back outside and Alex was STILL in the outhouse! I rapped on the door and told him to hurry up. All he said was, "I *will!*"

So, deciding to be *extremely* patient, I brought Bess *and* Walter from the pasture into the barn for milking. Before I started milking Bess I went back to the outhouse. "What are you doing, Alex?" I asked, still trying to be patient. Then he came out and told me he'd been looking for a certain toy in the Eaton's. I was so mad I yelled at him to just scram and go milk Walter. He did and when I got to the barn we didn't talk. Alex finished milking before me and when I got to the house Mother told me to sweep the floor and the porch and think about the meaning of patience while I did it. I couldn't help myself. I said, "Well, I find it VERY ANNOYING when people look at old Eaton's in outhouses when they don't have any business to do!" Mother told me to stop complaining and start sweeping and not to be so vulgar. It isn't vulgar, it's the truth!

THURSDAY, OCTOBER 13, 1927

I made the mistake today of saying in front of Mother how tedious it is to have a Spelling test EVERY week. "Emily, if you don't stop complaining, I will give you something real to complain about." That is exactly what she said. I think she was partly referring to last night.

I am so tired of having to hold in my complaints all the time. I wish I could just walk into the middle of the main street and scream them out. I would say things like this: I HATE IT WHEN . . .

–People have a nice leisurely look at the Eaton's in the outhouse
–I have Spelling tests every week
–Grown-ups don't let me have my say
–Relatives (especially those whose names begin with *M*) invite themselves to visit without giving an exact date
–I have to clean up after Alex
–My bed creaks every time I roll over
–My own family, along with the entire town, keeps mysterious things about my uncle a secret from me

I feel better now, but I wonder if complaining is a sin that I'll have to tell Father Duquette at Confession.

FRIDAY, OCTOBER 14, 1927

Not a lot happened today. Oh — one interesting thing is that Mother sent me down to the store to get more waterglass so we can keep the eggs fresh for the winter and just after I left I saw Joe walk into the store with Millie Ross! I wonder if he is sweet on her or if he was just being friendly. I will have to pay closer attention.

Sunday, October 16, 1927

I am in trouble and it's all because of Millie Ross. All right, I *wish* it were because of Millie Ross. After supper I was drying the dishes and Joe was sitting at the table reading. I asked him if he knew how Millie Ross was keeping these days. Without looking up he said, "I don't know. Fine, I guess. I saw her yesterday on my way into the store. Why?" I knew by this reply that he wasn't sweet on her but I wasn't going to stop trying to tease when I had already put my mind to it. So I said, "A little bird told me you are sweet on her!" (I said this in what I meant to be a very annoying singsong voice.) Joe looked up and laughed. "You're just trying to get my back up, you little squirt!"

I said, well what if I was, and I threw the towel at him and jumped to one corner of the kitchen. Joe sprang at me but I ran out of the corner and then he chased me around the table a couple of times. I ran out of the kitchen squealing and I heard Mother call from the parlour to settle down, but we didn't of course. I ran up the stairs yelling "Millieeeee" and then I flew into my room and jumped on my bed, which made a very awful, very loud cracking sound.

Me and Joe both froze on the spot. Then my bed caved in! It turns out that me jumping onto it broke some of the boards underneath, which made the whole thing cave in. And now I'm in trouble for it. It isn't my fault! Everyone knows that that bed has been in our family for thousands of years. If I had a metal bed frame like everyone else, it wouldn't have broken. I guess I should have mentioned the creaking to Pa when it started a while back.

Now Joe laughs every time he looks at me. Ha Ha Ha. He's not the one who has to camp out on his bedroom floor until his bed gets fixed. Mother would say not to complain. I've decided that complaining in here doesn't count as complaining. It's more like expressing my woes. Pa told me to try to make the best of my situation. I think I will pretend that I am Anne of Green Gables sleeping in a spare room.

———————————

I am just about to put out the lamp, and there's a big row happening because Alex wants to camp out on his floor but Mother won't let him. She says he'll catch a cold. She doesn't seem to be very worried about *me* catching a cold. 'Night.

MONDAY, OCTOBER 17, 1927

I survived my first night of indoor camping. I'm not even all that sore. Last night after five minutes of arguing, Alex finally stopped trying to convince Mother to let him sleep on the floor. When I went into the boys' room this morning to wake Alex up, where was he? Sleeping on the floor, of course! I pretended not to notice and I decided not to tell Mother.

Oh yes — I am keeping this book in my dresser drawer again, just until my bed is fixed.

WEDNESDAY, OCTOBER 19, 1927

Pa told us at supper today that he will be leaving for a lumber camp in Témiscaming in a week. We all got quiet for a little bit. No one likes to see him go, but we all know that it's part of his work, since you can't farm in the winter. At least he isn't taking Whinny and Wilfrid to work in the camps like some of the other men do with their horses. Pa brought them one year, when he was working closer to Mattawa, and I missed them terribly.

THURSDAY, OCTOBER 20, 1927

Pa and Joe had a bit of an episode today, which I only saw because Alex, Will and I were playing hide-and-seek. I was hiding in the barn loft, covered in straw, when I heard someone come into the barn. I peeked through the hole that Alex and I had discovered in the floor, and saw that it was Pa, come to get some oil. Joe came in not four seconds after Pa, and I heard him say he'd really like to go to Témiscaming with Pa this winter.

I won't repeat the whole thing here, but it blew up into the biggest argument. I have never heard Joe so angry, and he even said the four-letter D-word, which I have never heard him say before. That seemed to make Pa more angry than anything, and he said in a terrifyingly calm voice, "You will not swear while you live under my roof. And until you can learn to control your impulsive outbursts of anger, you can forget about coming to Témiscaming." Then I'm quite sure Pa left because he disappeared from my view and a minute later Joe gave a mighty yell and I heard him punch the wall. But soon he stopped and left too. He was as calm as anything at supper and since then he's been very quiet. I'm sure he is wishing he could go with Pa.

FRIDAY, OCTOBER 21, 1927

I talked with Pa about the L.C.M. today. He had just put the finishing touches on my bed when I came up to show him my perfect score on today's Spelling test. He sat on the bed and looked at the test and said how proud he is of me.

Then my question just burst out. I asked him what had happened to Uncle Mathieu in the camps. Pa looked genuinely confused and asked what had put an idea like that into my head. I said Miss Adams had. He sort of smiled. "Emily, you know better than to listen to anything Miss Adams says about our family, or anyone else's for that matter. We all know that she enjoys gossip and tends to mix up the names and events of reality!"

What could I reply to that? Maybe Miss Adams wanted to appear as though she knows what's happening in everyone's families, or maybe her memory is fooling her.

Saturday, October 22, 1927

We waterglassed lots and lots of eggs today. This year, Mother taught me how to do the entire task from beginning to end, instead of just getting me to help her with individual parts. It's a pretty boring job but I'm always thankful to have the eggs for baking in the winter, especially at Christmas. To get the eggs ready you have to make sure they don't have any cracks in them. Then you have to place them very carefully, layer by layer, in a stone crock. You can't just put them in any which way, because then they'll take up more room, or they'll move and crack. After this, you boil one gallon of water. Once it's cool, you add sixteen ounces of waterglass to the water and stir the mixture together. Then you have to pour the concoction into the crock and make sure that it covers all of the eggs. Last, you cover the crock with a cloth and its lid and put it in the cellar to keep it cool.

This last step was the worst part, because this year, for the first time, *I* had to carry the eggs to the cellar. It was tricky because the cellar stairs are so steep and it is dark and I couldn't see the steps in front of me because the crock blocked them. But I managed not to drop any of the crocks and they're sitting safely on some crates down there.

Sunday, October 23, 1927

I have news: Auntie Annabelle and Uncle Mathieu came for supper tonight and Auntie told us that she is expecting a *baby*! It is supposed to come sometime in April.

Well! I feel as though I am turning into one of those adults who never seems to remember fun things, but only concerns herself with mundane daily tasks! Hallowe'en is in only a week! I had thought of it a few weeks ago, but then I became so distracted with Auntie Mai's letter and Joe's birthday and my bed breaking and Auntie Annabelle's news that I completely forgot about it. I wonder when I would have thought of it if Will hadn't reminded me. We were walking home from school and he said, "What are you going to be next Monday, Em?" I thought it was some kind of riddle, so I said, "I don't know, what?" He gave me a strange look. "For *Hallowe'en*, Em!" said Alex.

I must have looked extremely amazed because Will said to me, incredulously (Spelling word), "You *forgot* Hallowe'en?"

We went to the store and Will showed us his costume. It's so fancy! I don't know exactly what he is supposed to be, but I suppose it doesn't matter, as long as it's mysterious and scary. His costume is all black and it comes with a mask and he even has a black cape. Alex and I will be ghosts. We have always been ghosts, and always will be, I suppose. Last year I asked Mother why we couldn't be something more interesting, something that involved more than a bedsheet. She said it was because we would be breaking an age-old Bilodeau tradition if we weren't ghosts. I know that isn't true, because when Mother was young, nobody dressed in costumes for Hallowe'en. Many children still don't. I think the real reason is that she doesn't have the time to make elaborate costumes. Still, her answer made me smile.

WEDNESDAY, OCTOBER 26, 1927

Pa has left for Témiscaming. He was gone before I got up for school this morning. He leaves early to make sure he gets there with a good amount of daylight left and has time to get "settled in." He took the train to Témiscaming and will walk out to the camp. I miss him already.

Joe doesn't seem upset or anything, even though he says Andrew constantly talks about what day he will leave. I still wish Pa had told us why he is so set against Joe going to the bush. But I'm also sort of tired of thinking about the L.C.M. I wish someone would just explain all of these mysteries to me!

THURSDAY, OCTOBER 27, 1927

I cannot write much tonight. I turned the cream separator for an hour and then churned for just as long because Mother is salting butter so we can have some during the winter even if the cows are calving. Mother separates and churns almost every morning and evening, so I guess I shouldn't complain. And Mother pays me to help with the separating since she sells some of the cream to a creamery in Renfrew. I can't complain about that, either.

When I finally finished separating, she took our ghost costumes out of the trunk in her room and let us try them on. I have to wear Joe's old one this year because mine from last year is too short, and the last time Joe went trick-or-treating he was my age, so his fits me almost perfectly. It's a little long, but I think it adds effect. For the last few years Joe hasn't asked for tricks or treats, he has just gone around town with Andrew and the older boys to cause mischief. I've asked him which pranks he played but he always says he can't tell me. I thought of threatening him with the roof-jumping incident, like Will said he might do to Andrew, but I didn't. Joe has never treated me like an annoying little kid and I don't want to make him start now.

SATURDAY, OCTOBER 29, 1927

I have such a story to tell! This is the kind of thing that only happens in books, and never to a real person, and yet it happened to none other than Emily Marie Pattersen of the Pembroke Road, Mattawa, Ontario! Yesterday was so normal and boring and all day I had been wondering what I could write about in my entry, and nothing came up. That's why I didn't write. Well, something did end up happening, but so late that I didn't have the time or energy to write.

I should start by saying that Joe spent last night at the Robertses' house because he was going to help Andrew and Mr. Roberts deliver a big order that was due very early this morning. Anyhow, I guess it was around midnight or later, and I was dreaming that I was in Témiscaming, standing on part of the frozen lake beside the cream separator. I was trying to turn the crank but it was stuck. Then Joe showed up and said I was being silly and he pulled my ghost costume out of the separator! Then Pa came running up yelling our names and telling us to get off the ice or we would drown.

Pa's voice became Mother's and I realized Mother was shaking me awake (this is no longer the dream). "Emily, quick! Put on something warm and run over to the Robertses' and get Joseph. Bess is sick."

Have you ever awakened in the middle of the night and set about doing something while you were half asleep, only to suddenly wake right up and realize that you still have a few hours of sleep left? And you come upon your unfinished job the next day and wonder how you ever did such excellent work at that time of the night without even knowing you were doing it? Well, that has happened to me once before, and it happened again last night. I didn't think about anything much except that Bess was sick and I had to go get Joe. I slipped my drawers on under my nightgown and I pulled on my boots, coat, hat and mittens and ran out the door and down the road. It was COLD! I woke up as I ran, and believe me, I was wide awake by the time I got to the store. It was a good thing the moon was out because I didn't have a lantern. All was quiet there, of course, and I went around the back to knock on the door that leads to the house instead of the store. I felt really foolish about waking everyone up just to get Joe. That's when I got the swell idea that maybe I could sneak in and get Joe without waking anyone else up.

I had to go eat supper and do the dishes and then help Alex practise his reading, but back to my story!

Anyway, at that point I remembered once overhearing

Mr. Roberts tell Pa that he keeps a spare key at the back of the house, beside the porch stairs, under an egg-shaped stone. I found the stone and looked under it. The key WAS NOT THERE! I climbed the back porch stairs and tried the door. It was UNLOCKED. I thanked God in my head but then I felt scared because I thought that if the key was gone and the door was unlocked, maybe there was a thief already somewhere inside. I bravely carried on, thinking how glad I was that I have been upstairs in that house enough to know my way around in the dark.

I climbed the stairs, and even though I tried to be quiet, they creaked so much that I was amazed no one came running. You would not believe how loud creaking stairs sound in the middle of the night when you're sneaking around someone else's house! I may as well have yelled "INTRUDER!!!!!" with every step I took. I got to the top, and was just passing Will's door on my way to Andrew's when something jumped at me, pushed me to the floor, and yelled, "THIEF, PA!"

I screamed at the same time as the person yelled and I realized that it was Will who had got me! I was so angry, scared, surprised and embarrassed that I kicked him and whispered, rather unkindly, "For Goodness' *sakes* Will, it's *me*." I guess I didn't sound like myself because he never replied, but kept me pinned there while he yelled for his Pa and I kept struggling. Soon everyone had rushed to the landing to see what was going on. Joe's face appeared, lit by a lamp, and I said, "Ma needs you! Bess is sick." I saw him hand the lamp to Andrew and at the same time, Will jumped up in amazement. Mr. Roberts had the presence of mind to turn on an electric light, and he seemed to realize what had happened and he rushed off after Joe. Mrs. Roberts came over to me and helped me off the floor.

"I'm sorry," I said. "I was having a dream about me and Joe and the cream separator when Mother woke me up and said to put something warm on and to come get Joe because Bess is sick and I didn't want to wake anyone else up but I guess I did anyway . . . " I said that all in one breath and faded to a stop. Mrs. Roberts said it was fine. She was speaking in a kind voice, but it didn't make me feel any less foolish. "Let's go downstairs and have some cocoa," she said. "Then William can walk you home."

We did go downstairs and have some cocoa, but I fidgeted because I wanted to go see if Bess was all right. I apologized for scaring them and waking them up. Mrs. Roberts kept insisting not to worry about it, but Will didn't say anything. I thought he was angry at me for kicking him, so I apologized. He blushed and said he was the one who should be apologizing for jumping at me. Ha! It was nice to see him blush for a change.

Will walked me home as soon as we finished the cocoa, and by the time I arrived Uncle Mathieu was there and was looking after Bess. Alex had been sent to get him since Alex was the one who heard Bess's mooing on his way to the outhouse. Mother had sent me to get Joe in the hopes that he would get to the house sooner and could do something to help Bess while Uncle Mathieu was on his way, but Joe and Mr. Roberts didn't arrive much ahead of him anyway. Mr. Roberts and Will drove home and Mother sent me back to bed. I slept in this morning and woke up at nine o'clock.

Sunday, October 30, 1927

Bess is doing much better. I think something got into her stomach but Uncle Mathieu says she'll be fine.

Will explained to me today that the spare key for his house was gone because once the frost comes his father hides the key under the windowsill beside the back door so that it doesn't get stuck under the stone when it freezes to the ground. And the snow comes soon too, which will bury the stone. I asked why the door was unlocked and Will said that his father had asked him to lock it but he forgot. I suddenly realized what this might mean for Will — I asked if he was given trouble. "Not really," he said, grinning. "Just a fair licking and sent to bed without supper; nothing I couldn't endure."

Ha Ha Ha.

Monday, October 31, 1927

Joe is gone, and we don't know where he is.

I was the one to notice, because when I went to the boys' room to wake Alex up for school, Joe wasn't there. I found it odd because just last night I heard him telling Mother that he didn't have any work to do for anyone in town today so he might sleep a little later. At first I thought he might be outside in the barn checking on Bess, but when Alex and I went out to milk Bess and Walter, he wasn't there. He wasn't anywhere outside. All we could think of was that maybe he was at Andrew's. Mother told me to leave for school early and stop by the Robertses' to ask about him while she finished getting Alex ready. I was supposed to tell Joe to go straight home if he was there and then I was to go to school.

It was Will who answered the door. He was holding his speller in one hand and a spoon in the other. He grinned and told me that I was too early and to come back in ten minutes. Very funny. He let me in and Mrs. Roberts came over from the stove and took my coat and invited me to sit down. I asked if they'd seen Joe. They hadn't.

Now I was getting worried. He hadn't gone there to see Andrew because Andrew had just left for Témiscaming. "I'm sure he'll show up before the day is through," Mrs. Roberts told me, "and if he comes here this morning, I'll send word to you at dinner." She knew I was upset because she gave me a little hug and patted me on the head. I felt like a little kid, and I almost started crying. I probably would have if Will hadn't been there. I was determined not to cry in front of a boy.

Mrs. Roberts offered me some milk but I said no thank you, and to distract myself I sat at the table testing Will on our new Spelling words while he finished his porridge. Mrs. Roberts had to tell him to hurry up three times and when I started to put my coat back on Will began shovelling the rest of his porridge into his mouth really fast. I had been hoping that Joe and

Alex were the only boys in the world who do that. He grinned at his mother's look of disapproval and her "Smarten up, William Roberts! We have company!" I smiled a little. "Don't encourage him, Emily," sighed Mrs. Roberts. I know she was teasing — they both wanted to cheer me up.

I was in a gloomy mood for the rest of the day. I tried to act normally, but I kept thinking about Joe. Even Tilly asked me if something was wrong. I told her I guessed I was just tired.

No word came from Mrs. Roberts at dinner, and Will and Alex walked ahead on the way home and "left me to my thoughts," as Mother would say. I don't know why Alex isn't more upset. I guess he just lets things happen without worrying so much. I wish I could do that.

When I got home Mother said she'd noticed some of her biscuits and the leftover roast beef were gone. This means that Joe must have planned to leave and probably means to stay away for a few days or more. Oh, Joseph Pattersen, you mischievous, beloved brother! Why couldn't you at least have left a note?!

———————

After supper me and Alex and Mother and Uncle Mathieu each went around town asking about Joe. When I asked Mr. Rankin if he had seen him, he gave me a very mysterious answer. He said, "Well now, all I have to say is that Joe is safe and off to do what a young man his age has to do." It seemed quite clear to me: Joe took the train and has followed Pa and Andrew to Témiscaming.

I told Mother and Uncle what Mr. Rankin said and they agree with my theory. They rushed to the station to try to learn more from Mr. Rankin, but all he would say was that he saw Joe getting on the train but didn't know where he was going to get off. Now Mother can't wait for Pa's first letter so she knows the address of his camp and can write to ask him about Joe.

I don't want to go out for Hallowe'en, but I think I will anyway because I can imagine what Will would have to say to me if I didn't. Maybe it will help keep me from thinking too much about Joe.

TUESDAY, NOVEMBER 1, 1927
All Saints' Day

We said special prayers in school this morning because it is All Saints' Day, and I prayed specially for Joe.

I'm glad I went out for Hallowe'en after all — it was fun! I got lots of apples and peppermints and cookies and toffee! Will and Alex kept trying to scare each other, but it was difficult for them to do because we were all walking together. I tripped over my costume twice and the bottom of the sheet is very dirty. Our outhouse got tipped over but Uncle Mathieu stopped by and righted it this morning before he started work. Mr. Roberts' store windows got soaped and someone even stole a wheel from Miss Adams's buggy! It was lying across the street from her house. I guess the boys weren't mean enough to hide it on her.

Mother's patience is getting thinner by the day because Auntie Mai could show up any time now. She said to expect her in early November, and it is early November. Mother says that early November could be the third, or it could be the twelfth, depending on how you look at it. Both are early compared to the thirtieth! I feel bad for her and I try to help often without complaining. I think Mother has noticed this because before I came up to write in here, she thanked me for all of my hard work in school and at home. She doesn't do that often!

THURSDAY, NOVEMBER 3, 1927

The chickens aren't laying many eggs now because the days are too short. Mother is saving the nicest ones and we'll waterglass them as a final batch on Friday after school. That way they'll be as fresh as possible when we want to use them for baking. (I used to wonder why we don't fry or poach them, until Mother told me that you mostly use waterglassed eggs for baking.)

I guess Pa is letting Joe stay in Témiscaming. That is good. I hope Joe writes soon.

FRIDAY, NOVEMBER 4, 1927

It is snowing! It snowed yesterday too but not very much. Today the flakes were falling thick and fast and there is already about a foot! Alex and I are very excited and I am happy for Pa and Joe too because I've heard that snow makes it easier to work with the logs in the bush.

I wonder what Joe's job is in the camp. And I wonder what Pa had to say when Joe showed up.

I can't go outside to play until this next batch of eggs is waterglassed. Alex agreed to milk Bess and Walter both, and to feed Whinny and Wilfrid *and* the chickens to make my job go faster, because Mother said we can go play after those jobs are done. Alex isn't always bothersome!

SATURDAY, NOVEMBER 5, 1927

Auntie Mai is here and SHE BROUGHT THE COUS-INS! Will came tearing up our lane and found me and Alex in the barn, milking Bess and Walter. "I think your aunt is here," he panted. "She brought your cousins too, I think." Will had been helping Mr. Rankin at the station and he heard her name spoken and saw that she had two children with her, so he figured it was her. Will snuck away so that Mother wouldn't know he had come. I suppose that we should have told her what Will had told us, but we didn't want to get Will in trouble for eavesdropping, even though it wasn't on purpose.

Anyhow, Auntie Mai told Mother that the teacher who was to look after the cousins is sick. Ha! Alex and I think that the old lady is very smart and is anything but sick. She probably knows all about the children's antics and is faking her illness. I think that is clever but self-ish, because now we have to put up with them! So the cousins are here, and missing school while they visit. Joe would call Auntie Mai a flat tire. It means that you come uninvited and spoil all the fun. The cousins are

Anne and Wilbur and they are so rude to Mother, Alex and me. Whenever they say something rude A.M. just tells them to "be nice to your auntie and your cousins, children!" I wish I were Joe right now.

Sunday, November 6, 1927

Last night I was trying to fall asleep but I could hear A.M. and Mother talking in the kitchen and I could not resist going to the top of the stairs to listen. A.M. plans to stay for two weeks! That is SO long!

Today at church Father Duquette spoke about Thanksgiving and Armistice Day, which are both tomorrow. No school! But Auntie and Co. are here. I hope they help prepare the meal. Auntie Annabelle and Uncle Mathieu are coming for supper, so we will have a full house. It would be even fuller if Pa and Joe were here. Pa says it is good that Thanksgiving and Armistice Day are on the same day because it reminds us that peace is something to be thankful for. Pa didn't fight in the Great War because the government said he was essential here and was to continue farming. He was glad about it. He didn't want to fight, especially since that would have meant leaving Mother alone with a baby (who was Joe!).

Today after Mass, Father Duquette announced that there will be a Church Social in about two weeks, on Saturday the nineteenth, as a late fundraiser to help pay for the new addition to the hospital. There will be a supper and a rummage sale and then dancing! I'm looking forward to it already.

MONDAY, NOVEMBER 7, 1927
Thanksgiving Day and Armistice Day
I don't have much time to write because I have to help in the kitchen. So far it appears as though our big family supper will run decently, in spite of the cousins being here.

———————————

Everything did run decently.

TUESDAY, NOVEMBER 8, 1927
Mother has had a letter from Pa! There is so much to tell. It was such an unusual letter, first because it was so long. We all know that Pa doesn't often write from the camps, and when he does his letters are very short.

But the things the letter said! Pa and Joe's arguments must have been bothering Pa because he started right out by telling us that he has explained to Joe why he didn't want him to go to the camps! He said that once he'd told him, Joe said that Pa should tell us too — we are a family, after all. It turns out that Pa's reason for wanting to keep Joe home *is* related to the L.C.M.! But it's not a happy mystery to have solved.

Miss Adams was right on the mark about what she said in the store that day: I *did* have an uncle who was hurt at the camps. But it wasn't Uncle Mathieu. It was a brother of Pa's who I had never heard of, and his name was Thomas. He was a lot older than Pa, because Pa's father's first wife died and Grandfather remarried. Uncle Thomas came to Canada in the summer of 1876, when he was eighteen. That winter he got involved in some lumbering operations near Pembroke. The spring after he arrived in Canada, he was working on a log drive and drowned while he was trying to free a log-jam. Pa said that Uncle Thomas's death in Canada was part of the reason he decided to come here — he wanted to feel closer to his brother.

I'm glad Pa has finally explained to us what's been going on. It doesn't sound like Pa is angry at Joe either, which is a relief. And now we all know that Joe is safe and sound with Pa. I'm glad they talked about the L.C.M.!

I also know about having an Uncle Thomas now, which is good, even though it's sad at the same time.

There is so much to think about.

Pa's letter had one thing to make me sad (Uncle Thomas) and one thing to make me happy (his not being angry with Joe). And now another thing has happened to make me happy: Auntie Mai has changed her mind and is only staying for one week! I think it's because she doesn't like it on the farm. Yesterday Mother asked her to collect the eggs (the hens are still laying a little) and she looked very surprised and said, in a simply dripping voice, "Of *course*, Anastasie, dear! What's a *farmhouse* without eggs?" And she hates using the outhouse. Uncle Timothy has indoor plumbing in Pembroke. When she arrived on Saturday she asked Mother where she and Pa had installed the water closet and scowled when Mother laughed and said it was still in the backyard. I don't understand why Auntie acts this way — she is Mother's sister! She grew up on this very farm, collecting eggs and milking cows and using the outhouse, the same as Mother! Maybe she is like Amelia's mother and is used to city life now.

WEDNESDAY, NOVEMBER 9, 1927

The cousins are so rude. They complain about the food and the beds even though we have given them Joe's and Alex's beds! They say they are lumpy and scratchy. We have even given A.M. Mother's bed. Alex has mine and Mother and I are sleeping on the floor on our ticks! We could let the Relatives sleep in the spare room but Mother says it's too much trouble to have to heat, especially since they are not staying much longer. I am beginning to think that Mother is not willing to go out of her way for A.M. I think she is annoyed.

The cousins are UNBELIEVEABLE. I even dare to say that I might find it more tolerable to live with Tilly. I am very sure *she* would never RIP PAGES OUT OF MY SPELLER. I was sitting in the parlour reading, Alex was at his friend's house, Mother had gone to close up the barn for the night, and Auntie Mai was napping by the fire. I could hear that Anne and Wilbur were in the kitchen, and they were being fairly quiet, except that every couple of minutes it sounded as though one of them had stumbled, and they would both laugh. After the third burst of laughter I got suspicious and went to see what they were doing. I arrived in time to see them playing tug-of-war WITH MY SPELLER. "Stop it, you two!" I yelled. In the next instant Mother came in from the barn, Auntie Mai appeared in the doorway behind me, Anne won the tug-of-war, and Wilbur fell on the floor, holding a page of my speller and laughing so hard his face was turning purple.

I was speechless and I looked to Mother for help. Then I felt tears of frustration welling up in my eyes. I didn't want the cousins to see me cry, so I ran up to my room. I had just finished having a good cry when I heard a knock on my door. I thought it must be Mother, but it turned out to be Auntie Mai with the cousins, who rhymed off the most insincere apology I have ever heard.

The only good thing of it all is that when I went downstairs to help Mother pack the lunches, Mother told Auntie Mai that she expected the cousins to paste the page back into my speller. To which Auntie Mai said, "Oh! Of course, Anastasie! I understand that Anne and Wilbur must take the blame." Mother said she was glad Auntie understood and that the paste was in the drawer, if they would be so kind as to do that now.

You should have seen Auntie's face! It didn't take her long to replace her astonished expression with a tight-lipped one as she got the paste from the drawer. Then she sat down at the table and fixed the speller herself!

Thursday, November 10, 1927

I feel sorry for Mother for having to spend all day with Auntie and Co. and am also very glad that I can escape to school. Thank Goodness Auntie Mai hasn't decided to send Anne and Wilbur with us. I get ready for school quickly and take my time walking home, and I stop at the store every day. I don't know if Mother has noticed.

Friday, November 11, 1927

I know now that Mother has been aware of my dawdling after school all week because today when I came in she pointedly looked at the clock and then raised her eyebrows at me. She smiled as she did it, though, and didn't say anything, so I think she was just letting me know that she knew what I had been up to. At least they leave tomorrow.

Saturday, November 12, 1927

Happy Thought
by Robert Louis Stevenson

The world is so full of a number of things,
I'm sure we should all be as happy as kings.

That is a poem from my copy of A *Child's Garden of Verses* and it could not be more true right now, because Auntie Mai, Anne and Wilbur are gone!

It is such a joy to sleep in my very own bed again.
I have to go now because it's bath time.

Monday, November 14, 1927

Oh no! I had a letter from Joe today. This whole thing is turning out VERY BADLY after all. For me anyway. After school Alex ran off to the store with Will, Clarence and Thomas Wilson because Will had something to show them and they said it was top secret, so I went to the post office by myself. Usually Alex and I get the mail together and sometimes Mr. Meredith gives us a piece of gum to split.

Anyhow, today Mr. Meredith said that yes, there was an envelope for me. As soon as he handed it over I recognized the writing as Joe's. And I noticed that the postmark said *Temagami*, not *Témiscaming*. At first I thought I read it wrong, because Pa had said in his letter that Joe was with him in Témiscaming. But my heart started to sink as I realized that Pa didn't actually *say* that in his letter. He just said that he'd explained the L.C.M. to Joe — he didn't say *when!* He must have told Joe all about it before he even left for Témiscaming.

I began to wonder what Joe was up to. I moved towards the door as Mr. Meredith turned to help some others who had come in, and right then and there I ripped open the envelope. There were three letters in it. One was for Mother and two were for me. And the ones for me were full to the brim of things to make my head spin. No sense in me describing what Joe said. I'll just paste the letters in, and that will ensure that Mother will never find them. She would never look in my journal without my permission.

November 4, 1927

Dear Emily:

You can breathe easy now, little sister, I'm fine! I guess you've already seen by the postmark that I'm in Temagami and not Témiscaming. But don't blurt anything out just yet. Read this letter first and see why I want to keep it a secret.

First, I don't want anyone to worry. As far as Mother knows, I'm in Témiscaming with Pa, and as far as Pa knows, I'm at home with you and Mother and Alex.

I'm where I want to be and I don't want anyone trying to make me go someplace else. I want to start making my own way and I decided to begin by spending this winter in the camps, without being given any trouble. I'll do all the explaining when the time comes.

So please don't tell anyone where I am. Just go along as if you had this letter from me in Témiscaming. I've written a very ordinary letter to Mother. No one should find out because I know that you and Alex pick up the mail after school, and Mother and Pa don't write much.

It's one thing to hear Pa describe the camps, but something else to actually be here.

Most of us wake up at quarter to six in the morning

and eat bacon, beans and tea for breakfast. The food is good and there's always plenty. I found a dead fly baked into my bread a few days ago, though. The boy sitting next to me (Jack) told me just to cut it out with my knife.

After breakfast we go into the bush in our gangs. I'm in gang two with Jack. I recognize some of the men in camp, but he's one of the only ones who's around my age and who I know from home. He's worked in the camps every winter since he was eleven, so he knows everything about them.

Every gang has about five men who have different jobs. There's the teamster (drives the horses), roller (rolls the logs onto the skidway), log makers (experienced men who cut the trees), and I'm the trail cutter. Jack said that someone who does my job is called the swamper, but trail cutter sounds better. I want to be a teamster but I'm not experienced enough yet. Some day.

On the first day in the bush Mr. Mackey and Mr. Boutz decided where to start cutting. We cleared an area for the skidway (where we pile the logs for the winter, before we take them to the lake), made a trail for the horses, and cleared around the big trees so they'd be easier to get at.

After the clearing was done we cut two big logs to use as skids for our skidway. Once it was built Mr. Boutz and Mr. Mackey started cutting the trees down with the Swedish fiddle (that's the crosscut saw). Once a tree falls we use axes to limb it, and then we hook the log up to the horses and Jack drives them to the skidway. The logs are easy to roll onto the skidway at first, but once we start getting more, we have to pile them higher to save room.

My first day, we stopped for dinner and built a fire to make toast and tea and warm up some beans. We worked until the shadows were long, and Mr. Mackey said we should start heading back to camp. Just as the buildings came in sight, I heard this awful loud banging and clanging and looked at Jack, who told me it was the gut iron, calling us all in for supper. That's what they call the dinner triangle.

Before Mr. Boutz eats he has to report to the clerk about how many logs our gang cut so that if there's some disagreement when McMillan's scalers come to scale the logs, they can look it all up. I haven't seen Mr. McMillan here, but Jack says McMillan trusts the Push (that's the foreman) to keep everything running smoothly.

For supper tonight we had salt pork, potatoes and carrots, and for dessert there were apple and raisin pies. There's a sign nailed to the wall inside the dining hall that says: NO SWEARING. NO SPITTING. From what I've heard so far, they need that sign!

After supper everyone has a bit of time to themselves to tell stories or write home or play cards. Mother wouldn't be too happy with some of the language that comes out during the card games. I haven't seen anyone cheating yet. Sometimes Mr. Mackey plays his guitar and another man joins in with his fiddle.

I have to stop now because the choreboy just came in

and yelled, "Ten to nine!" He puts the lamps out in ten minutes, and Mr. Finnigan still has to lead us in prayers.

Bye for now,
Joe

Well, a good thing about Joe sending letters in a package addressed to me is that his letters to Mother won't have a postmark. Of course he would have thought of that.

But what if Mother writes separate letters to Joe *and* Pa at Témiscaming? I can't just send a letter from Mother to Joe in Témiscaming when I know very well he's in Temagami. I have no solution to this and my poor head cannot come up with one right now. I will think about it and hope to Goodness that Mother feels no need to write to Joe apart from Pa. And that she never wonders why their letters don't come together. Maybe she'll figure that Pa and Joe aren't reconciled about Joe being at camp after all, especially if Joe never mentions Pa in his letters.

The worst thing of all is that Joe's letter to Mother *was* perfectly normal, just like he said. It is much shorter than the one he wrote to me, and judging by Mother's reaction to it, he leaves the impression that he is plugging away next to Pa in Témiscaming. He told her about the food and what he does in the evenings. She doesn't seem worried that he didn't mention Pa.

I'm probably right — she must think that they aren't speaking. Which I am sure they wouldn't be if they were at the same camp. Pa must have thought that his explanation about Uncle Thomas would make Joe understand why he should stay home. I can just imagine how angry he'd be if he knew that Joe has disobeyed him after all of that!

And there is *another* problem! What if Mother ever does ask about Joe in her letters to Pa?

This is horrid. I can't go around reading Mother's letters to Pa before I mail them, can I? And if I ever did find a mention of Joe, what would I do?

What a stubborn, impulsive person! Joe hasn't thought this whole thing out very well, and if he has then it was pretty mean of him to go ahead and do it and put me in such a spot! I might as well paste his second letter in now, and then see if I can think of a solution.

November 5, 1927

Dear Emily:

I didn't have much trouble falling asleep last night! This work keeps me dog-tired and I'm finally used to all the snoring.

Lots of things about camp are different, and the toilet is one of them. The outhouse is really just wooden poles sitting above holes in the ground. That's all there is to sit on. There aren't full walls and it's all covered by a slanted roof.

The bunkhouses are a little crowded. They've all got a stove in the middle, with twine hanging from the ceiling all around. It smells pretty bad at the end of the day when everyone comes in and hangs their socks to dry. We hardly ever bathe, either. If you want me to live a long and happy life, DO NOT TELL MOTHER THAT!

Our beds are like at home, but we just have grey wool blankets for covers. Jack told me to be thankful that there aren't any bedbugs. One year he ended up in a scrappy camp where he had to spread coal oil on the tick to keep the bedbugs away, but then he'd go home smelling like coal oil. His mother didn't let any of his family touch him until he had a bath and changed clothes, and she'd boil all his things to keep the nits from hatching in the house.

I hope this letter wasn't boring, but I know you always want details. Has Auntie Mai come yet? How are Whinny and Wilfrid and Bess and Walter and the chickens? I'll see you at Christmas! And let me know what you've decided about our secret.

Love from,
Joe

P.S. The mail goes out from here so seldom that I'll save up my letters and send them out in a package once in a while. I didn't think I'd like to write so much but I want to tell you about my adventures, since I can't tell anyone else. Has Pa written with any mention of why he doesn't want me in the camps? I told him I thought the whole family should know about it.

———————————

I have decided to tell Mother the truth. I can't keep a dreadful secret like this! Especially not after what Pa told us about Uncle Thomas, and that because of what happened to him, Pa doesn't want Joe in the camps.

But what if Joe is right and this is how a person starts making his own way in the world? He is sixteen, after all.

I haven't told Mother.

There doesn't seem to be much to do other than agree to keep Joe's Dreadful Secret. What he said about everyone thinking he is safe and sound, right where they expect him to be, is true. What a commotion I would cause by telling the truth! And it is not that I am lying by not telling, I suppose. It is more like withholding bits of the truth. Joe said he would explain everything anyway — I guess when he comes home for Christmas. It's his responsibility. And it's not my story to tell.

All right, I have resolved to keep the D.S. (Dreadful Secret). It can't be that difficult. Unless Mother picks up the mail when I've got a package of letters from Temagami. Or unless she writes to Joe. Or unless she asks Pa how Joe is . . .

Who am I trying to fool? It WILL be difficult. But I am still resolved to keep it. The worst that can happen is that I'll have to explain everything. No one can get hurt, I don't think.

But you can bet that I will be giving Joe what-for in my next letter to him. I don't understand why it was so impossible for him to tell everyone the truth before he left! He will just have to do it at Christmas. . . .

New worry: I hope Joe gets home for Christmas before Pa does, so he can explain it all without everyone worrying about where he is.

What a horrid, horrid mess. I have never almost-dreaded Christmas's approach before!

TUESDAY, NOVEMBER 15, 1927

Aha! I have at least figured out how to keep Mother from sending letters to Joe at Témiscaming. If Mother ever gives me a letter to mail to Témiscaming, I will innocently try to find out who she wrote to. If it turns out she has written to Joe, I will have to steam the envelope open and put the letter to Joe in a new envelope addressed to him in Temagami. When I write to Joe next I'll explain it all to him. It's certainly going to cost me in postage. But thank Goodness for my creamery money, and that I'm the one who takes care of the mail for our family. It does make it easier for me to sneak the letters around.

But it all makes me feel quite guilty. What else can I do, though? Mr. Roberts says that it's a soldier's duty to follow orders, not to question them. Well, this soldier may be following orders so far, but she's not very happy about it!

Wednesday, November 16, 1927

I wrote to Joe today. I told him I agree to keep the D.S. unless Mother or Pa asks me something like, "What lumber camp is Joe at?" I also told him that I will redirect Mother's letters to him in Temagami, but that I refuse to look at what she writes to Pa, so if the secret comes out because of something Mother writes to Pa, then it's Joe's problem!

I said that it's best he keep sending his letters in batches. It will be that much less likely that Mother will pick up a D.S. letter! I also told him that he will have my wrath to reckon with when he comes home at Christmas. And also that I love him.

Thursday, November 17, 1927

Everyone at school is talking about the Church Social. I am excited about it, but I wish Pa and Joe were here so I'd have someone to dance with. Maybe some of the boys from school will ask me. Mother said I can dance with *Alex*. Can you believe that? She gave me a meaningful look, so I suspect she wants me to do it to make it fun for him.

At least there is more to the Social than just the dance. Mother is baking doughnuts and I am making cookies to bring for the dessert and I am also donating one of my unused handkerchiefs to the rummage sale. Today at dinner Tilly was telling all the girls about the *bee-you-tee-full* doilies she has crocheted for the rummage sale. I could have crocheted doilies too if my father were a doctor and I was spoiled and I didn't live on a farm and have chores to do.

In truth, I probably would not have crocheted doilies, no matter my circumstances. I hate crocheting.

I asked Mother and she said I could wear my special-occasion dress to the Social! She is so sympathetic sometimes, and other times she is not at all. I don't understand it.

FRIDAY, NOVEMBER 18, 1927
The chickens have stopped laying for sure now. I had to use the eggs we waterglassed last spring for my cookies. I can't wait for the Social tomorrow night!

SATURDAY, NOVEMBER 19, 1927
The Social was the most fun I have had since the wagon rides with Will and Clarence! First was the supper. It was roast beef and mashed turnips and potatoes and corn, and it was delicious! I brought four dozen oatmeal cookies and they were all gone by the end of the evening. There were also pies and cakes and muffins and doughnuts for dessert. They set up the rummage sale as everyone was beginning dessert and they kept set up through the dancing.

Mr. Roberts played his guitar and Sam Wilson was on the fiddle and old Mr. Toby even played his mouth organ and the spoons (not at the same time). I sat out for the first two dances and then Mother made me dance with Alex. But other brothers and sisters were doing the same so it was all right. Mother was asked to dance a little — there were more women than men there because of men being away in the camps. After three dances with Alex I sat down and Will asked me to dance! I danced with him for a bit and then Clarence asked me for a dance too. I am surprised at what a good dancer he is! I didn't tell him I was surprised, of course.

I could feel Tilly's eyes on me every time I stepped onto the floor, and she positively stared at me when I danced with Walter Blake. I am sure she is sweet on him because she has been making eyes at him lately. Walter eventually asked Tilly to dance, so she doesn't have to worry about anything. I don't care what she thinks about my dancing, either. I had fun and Joe would say that's all that matters. I'm going to bed now because it is late and there is church tomorrow.

SUNDAY, NOVEMBER 20, 1927
Very tired today. At least I stayed awake during Mass!

MONDAY, NOVEMBER 21, 1927
Poor Mother! I noticed while she was cooking supper that she was having trouble using her right hand, so I asked her what happened and it turns out she bruised her knuckles on the washboard this morning. I tried

to be as helpful as I could with the dishes. Then I was doing my homework when I was startled by a yell from Mother. She had tried ironing with her left hand because it hurts her to bend the first three fingers on her right hand, but she wasn't very good at it, and she ended up burning her right hand with the iron just a moment after it came off of the stove. Alex told her to put butter on it but she didn't because she says that makes it hurt even more. I agree. She ran out and stuck it in the snow instead.

It's too bad that the iron is so heavy. Someone should invent a featherweight iron. I'm sure they would become rich.

TUESDAY, NOVEMBER 22, 1927

In school we are practising the proper way to write letters. We are learning salutations, like "To Whom it May Concern," and complimentary closings, like "Sincerely." I think that part is a silly waste of time. The only good thing about it is that we are given time in class to write a letter to whoever we want! I will write one to Joe.

WEDNESDAY, NOVEMBER 23, 1927

I experienced ten minutes of a squirming stomach today because there was a letter for Mother from Pa at the post office. How tempted I was to rip it up at the post office, run back onto the bridge, throw the pieces over the railing and let them float down the river! I felt sick the whole way home and as I passed the parlour on my way up to my room just now I saw Mother standing at the stove reading the letter. She looked concerned.

I don't know how, but I dared to ask Mother about the letter. Luck was with me and she told me what I really wanted to know straight off, without my having to fish around. She said Pa didn't mention Joe and she's concerned that they might still be angry with each other and not speaking.

As terrible as it sounds, I am glad. If Mother thinks Pa is angry with Joe and not speaking to him, maybe she won't ask Pa anything about him.

Pa closed this letter with "give my love to the children." As far as Mother knows, "the children" are Alex and me.

THURSDAY, NOVEMBER 24, 1927
Mother's hand is healing — she can bend her fingers and there is a scab over the burn.

FRIDAY, NOVEMBER 25, 1927
One month until Christmas! I wonder when we will begin working on the school Christmas Pageant. I hope it is soon.

This evening at supper I asked Mother if she would tell us some stories, and one of the ones she told us was about Gertrude Bernard. Gertrude's ancestors were Indians and she was born in 1906. My favourite thing about her is that when she was only fourteen she went to work in a lumber camp in Temagami! They say that's where she met Grey Owl. Gertrude and Grey Owl don't live around here anymore, so Mother doesn't know anything else about them.

Sometimes I wish I were brave enough to work in the camps. Most times though (like when Joe tells me about flies in the bread and dirty socks and a lack of real outhouses) I am content to be un-brave Emily Pattersen of the Pembroke Road in Meeting of the Waters, Ontario. I've never really thought until I wrote it out in English that I've been using an Ojibway word all this time!

SATURDAY, NOVEMBER 26, 1927
We went sledding today! There was a heavy snowfall last night so everything was perfectly fresh. Will came to get me and Alex after breakfast and we got Clarence and went to the Rosemount side and some others from school joined us. Even Tilly showed up and at first she acted almost completely amiable. Then a snowball that Alex aimed at me went astray and hit her square in the face! Everyone except Walter laughed and she went home pouting.

MONDAY, NOVEMBER 28, 1927
When Alex and I stopped in at the post office on the way home from school the Bangs children were in there

talking about their Christmas concert. I guess the public school started planning theirs today. I can hardly wait to begin ours. I would like to be an angel, preferably one with lines. Joe would say that I'm just going to have to hold my horses until Sister announces it.

I'm getting a little nervous about picking up the post. It's been two weeks since my first letters from Joe. Will he have a package of letters to send out every time the mail leaves camp? Or will he skip some? I had better make sure that from now until the secret comes out at Christmas, it is ALWAYS me and Alex who pick up the mail.

Thursday, December 1, 1927
Still no word about the Christmas Pageant. I'm afraid to ask Sister about it for two reasons, the first being that I don't want to seem too eager or else Tilly will act just as eager as me and try to get the part I want (even if I were to request being an animal), and the second being that Will is not excited about it at all and he said he'd put snow down my back if I reminded Sister of it. I think he was joking, but I don't want to take a chance. I told him he can hardly expect Sister to forget about the Pageant and he said didn't I know that Christmas was a season for miracles? I said that miracles weren't to be taken lightly. He threw a snowball at me and missed. Maybe Sister will announce it on Monday.

Friday, December 2, 1927

Sister announced the Christmas Pageant today! The morning went as usual, with Arithmetic and Spelling and Geography. Then in the afternoon, just before dismissal, she said that she supposed it was time to start working on the Pageant! The class immediately burst into an uproar and I knew why she had waited until a Friday afternoon to tell us. I looked across the aisle at Will and gave him what I think was a triumphant look. Sister got us all quieted down and said that this year we'll be having two pageants, one put on by the French side and one by the English side of the school, because if we had one big one with everyone in it, there would be "unreasonable numbers of sheep." I agree. She said that over the weekend we are to think about what part we might want to play so that we can tell her on Monday. The class of younger children is to do the same for Sister Bridget.

Sunday, December 4, 1927

I forgot to say that we had another letter from Pa, but it was short this time. I was breathless with suspense when I carried it home and handed it to Mother. We gathered around the kitchen table while she read it out loud, but it had no mention of Joe in particular! Just a bit about what the work and the food are like and that he thinks the pay is going to be pretty good this year.

I've just remembered that it is Will's birthday on the ninth — exactly three months after mine, only he is turning thirteen, not twelve. I'm saving my money for Christmas and postage, so I can't afford to buy him a gift. Besides, nothing I buy him at the store would be a surprise anyway. I'll have to think of something.

Monday, December 5, 1927

I was afraid that Sister would forget to ask us what we want to be in the Pageant but she didn't. At the end of the day everyone took turns telling her what part they'd like. I said I'd like to be an angel. To my surprise, Tilly said she'd like to be Mary. (Later, when we were all in the cloakroom getting ready to leave, she told every girl who would listen that her mother said that she is naturally solemn and innocent-looking). Will said that it didn't matter much to him what part he plays but that he doesn't want any lines. Alex told Sister Bridget that he would like to be a shepherd. I feel like Anne of Green Gables waiting to be told whether she will stay with the Cuthberts or not.

P.S. I have found Will's birthday present. I just have to get some final permission and fix it up a little and it will be set to go!

Tuesday, December 6, 1927

Will's present is ready. It's lucky I went to the train station with Will last night, because that's where I found it. We were in Mr. Rankin's office and Mr. Rankin was showing Will something on a map on the wall. They both had their backs to me and were completely absorbed in their conversation, so I began wandering around the office looking at things. I noticed an old striped conductor's cap hanging on a nail on the back of the door. I have never seen Mr. Rankin wearing it, and it looked a little ratty. I could see what I was sure was a hole near the back. I glanced over at conspirators Rankin and Roberts. They hadn't taken notice of me, and only Frankly saw me take the hat down and examine it more closely. But he didn't mind — he just blinked, closed his eyes, and started purring in his corner.

Anyhow, I was right — the hat did have a hole in it and it was dirty. I went back to the station today after supper, hoping to Goodness that Will wasn't there and wouldn't turn up. He didn't. I explained to Mr. Rankin why I wanted the hat and I asked him if I could barter for it. He agreed and said that he wouldn't say no to a batch of oatmeal cookies sometime, and a bit of cream for Frankly. I brought the hat home and washed it and patched the hole and it looks almost as good as new. I cannot wait to give it to Will.

WEDNESDAY, DECEMBER 7, 1927

I don't know if there is a happier person in the world right now. I got the part of the angel in the Pageant! I know Gabriel is supposed to be a boy, but Sister said she couldn't think of a boy who was willing to wear a white dress and a halo in public. Everyone giggled at that. Solemn-and-innocent-looking Tilly did get the part of Mary, but she certainly didn't look very innocent when Sister announced that Clarence would be Joseph! Clarence seems indifferent. I'm glad. I'd hate for the whole thing to be ruined for us all just because of Tilly. Will is the innkeeper and is happy with his few lines, and Alex is a shepherd.

THURSDAY, DECEMBER 8, 1927
MOTHER PICKED UP THE MAIL TODAY on her way home from Uncle Mathieu's. When Alex and I stopped in after school, Mr. Meredith, unaware of my predicament, told us that Mother had picked it up not an hour ago. Three parts of me wanted to do three different things. One wanted to start screaming and yelling at Mr. Meredith, asking him how he could do such a foolish thing as let Mother pick up the mail. Another part of me wanted so badly to rush home and make sure that there hadn't been a package from Joe, and the third part wanted to wander around Mattawa for the rest of my life without ever returning home in case Mother had figured out that Joe is not in Témiscaming. The part of me won that wanted to return home, except I didn't rush. There was nothing from Joe! Would I ever have dreamed that there would be a time when I would be happy to say that?

And: Happy News! Today on the way to school Will told me that for his birthday his mother is allowing him to invite some friends over for supper! He has asked me, Clarence and Thomas.

Friday, December 9, 1927

Supper at Will's was fine! I was the only girl there and at first I felt like I was holding the boys back from being . . . boys. But when Mrs. Roberts brought the cake in we all sang "For He's a Jolly Good Fellow" and Tom got the words mixed up. Everyone laughed and everything was fine from there. Clarence and Tom had put their money together to get Will something called a pogo stick. Tom's uncle is a banker and he sent Tom and his brother Timothy each one for their birthdays, but Timothy is sixteen and doesn't use his so Tom and Clarence bought it from him to give to Will. You should have seen it wrapped — I can imagine that it must have cost a fortune for Tom's uncle to send! The pogo stick is an odd-looking thing that is like a long stick that has handles at the top (almost like a bicycle), with two smaller sticks coming out of either side at the bottom, like this:

The smaller sticks are what you stand on. You are supposed to stand on these and jump, because the bottom of the long stick part has a spring in it.

It is VERY difficult to keep your balance. I asked Tom how to spell "pogo" because I knew I would be writing about it in here. He looked at me as though I had some contagious disease. "Why do you need to know that?" he asked, as though it were impossible for me to simply be *interested* in knowing. I explained about this journal. "I don't know," he said. "Who cares?"

Just like a boy. So I decided to spell it like it sounds. Anyway, I know Alex will love it when Will lets him try it. Will really liked my gift and he wore it for the entire evening!

SATURDAY, DECEMBER 10, 1927
Here I am, snuggled in my bed on this perfect, perfect winter morning. Well, it would be perfect if Pa and Joe were here and getting along. And if I didn't have to keep Joe's D.S. It snowed last night and I am just lying here, imagining all of the fun things I will do today, and taking my time about it so that I won't have to help Mary cook breakfast. I think I will lie here a while longer.

Alas, Mary had only just started cooking the bacon when I got downstairs. I do not have long to write because she gave me a list of things to get at the store. Then I am allowed to go sledding. I am sure that Will and Alex already have half the town outside flying down the hills with them.

I am back in bed. Sliding was fun. The boys can hardly wait for some good freezing weather so they can play hockey on our pond. I am looking forward to the pond too, but I can't skate on it because over the last year I have completely outgrown my skates. I will have to content myself with sliding on my boots until Christmas, when I HOPE I get a new pair of skates.

MONDAY, DECEMBER 12, 1927

A package of letters from Joe, and the Dreadful Secret is still safe! I gave Mother her letter from Joe. He even wrote a short note to Alex this time! Since there are several letters in the package, I've decided to savour them somewhat. I'll only paste one in every now and then, so that I can have a nice reminder of Joe once in a while. I'll have to keep the unread letters tucked in here, though, so Mother won't find them.

November 11, 1927

Hello Again, Sis!

Hope you can read the shaky hand. I cut my finger a while ago when I was sharpening my pencil. Jack had been hanging around me since supper, when I told him I couldn't play cards because I was going to write home. So he was with me when I cut my finger. He showed me how to make it heal faster by putting a bit of fir gum over it and singeing it and then blowing on it to cool it. He singed the gum a few times and said the cut should heal well.

Jack stuck around after he helped me with my cut, so I asked if he wanted something. He looked sort of uncomfortable but in the end he told me.

He can't read or write! When I said at supper that I was going to write to you, he followed me around so he could ask me to write a letter to his family. You should have seen him blush when he got to asking his sister to say hello to Sal Brooks for him!

Never thought the Sisters' dictations would come in handy in real life!

Joe

TUESDAY, DECEMBER 13, 1927

I *think* I am embarrassed — I don't really know what to think. At first, today was a perfectly normal day. I woke up, milked Bess, fed the pigs and chickens, met Will on the way to school, did lessons — everything was normal. Then after school Will and I were standing in the yard waiting for Alex, when Will said, "Emily, I can carry your books if you want," and his face turned quite red. At first I couldn't figure out why he thought I'd want him to carry my books and then I realized that he was *asking* me if he could carry them! I blushed too and was so flustered that at first I said, "No thank you," but then I realized that I wouldn't mind if he carried them. So I said, "Well, I suppose so," and handed them to him with a "thank you" just as Alex appeared at the top of the school stairs.

Alex grinned and said, "Well, I wish I had someone to carry *my* books!"

"*You're* my brother," I answered him. "You should be nice and carry mine sometime."

Saying this made me feel better and I think it lightened the air by about two million pounds. When we got home Alex blabbed to Mother, of course. I was afraid she'd tease but she smiled and said, "Well, Alex, why shouldn't anyone offer to carry Emily's books? William Roberts is a very nice boy."

The way people are going on about it, you'd think we are getting married or something.

Wednesday, December 14, 1927

I have bad news. Mother would say I'm exaggerating but I don't say so. As soon as I met Will on my way to school, he said he had a secret to tell me. I was excited because I thought it might have something to do with Pa (and Andrew) coming home for a visit. We had a hard time convincing Alex to run ahead to school but he finally did.

Before Will told me anything he made me swear not to tell anyone. I agreed unless it was something bad. He said it wasn't and he told me that last night he overheard his parents talking about leaving something at our house! He told me his pa said, "We can't let him find it so I'll bring it over to the Pattersens' in the morning." Will said he tried to hear more but his parents stopped talking. He told me he suspected that it was a Christmas present for himself. "So, Em, you have to look for it tonight." I asked him why I should waste my time looking for a gift of *his* that was *purposely* hidden at my house so he wouldn't see it, especially when I didn't even know what it was.

"Because if you don't, I'll sneak in in the middle of the night and look for it myself, only *I* won't make your stairs creak!" He grinned and OF COURSE I blushed. I said I'd think about it.

He risked coming to the girls' side of the yard at recess just to ask me what I had decided. I still don't know what to do. Will is my best friend, but I feel bad for ruining something that his parents want to be a surprise.

Why is it that *I* am always the one who has to decide whether to keep this secret and that secret; whether to tell the adults about this thing or that thing?

THURSDAY, DECEMBER 15, 1927
Will pestered me again today about the hidden thing. I told him that I wouldn't look for it specially but that if I found it I would tell him. He seemed satisfied, after making me cross my heart and hope to die, that I really would tell him if I found it. I hope Mother doesn't send me to the cellar for anything. If she does I'll just keep my mind on what I'm sent for.

FRIDAY, DECEMBER 16, 1927
The Pageant is coming along quite well. Everyone is scrambling to find costumes and scraps of things that

we can use to make the scenery. Here are my lines:

Fear not: for, behold, I bring you good tidings of great joy, which shall be to all people. For unto you is born this day in the city of David a Saviour, which is Christ the Lord. And this shall be a sign unto you; Ye shall find the babe wrapped in swaddling clothes, lying in a manger.

Then me and Jeanette and Martha (the other two angels) say, "Glory to God in the highest, and on earth peace, good will toward men."

At first I thought it would be difficult to memorize, but it is turning out not to be so hard. I'm going to practise a little and then go to bed.

SATURDAY, DECEMBER 17, 1927

The WORST thing just happened! I went to the barn loft to calm myself down after I found that Alex had eaten FIVE of my oatmeal cookies just before supper. I tripped over something buried in the hay and I crouched down and uncovered a brand new Fleet Wing sled with a fancy bow tied to the rope. For a moment I got SO excited and then I read the tag: *To William, Love, Ma and Pa.* I guess I'll have to tell Will tomorrow, or maybe I should wait until our walk to school on Monday, since it was on the way to school that he made me promise to tell him where it was, to begin with. Next thing you know he'll be asking me to sneak it over to his house in the middle of the night so he can try it out.

Sunday, December 18, 1927

Today is going by quite slowly so as a treat I decided to read another letter from Joe. I'll paste it in.

November 12, 1927

Em,

Today me and Jack were on our way to the lake to fish and we passed by a huge pine, and I mentioned to Jack that I was surprised no one had cut it down. He said it would be too dangerous and he pointed at the upper branches. They were all dead, and there were broken limbs caught in the branches the whole way down. He said they call those limbs widow-makers because they can fall and kill you, especially once you cut the tree and it starts to sway. He's seen it happen.

Another thing. Once I'd been here for a couple weeks I noticed that some of the older men were fussing about how they put their boots on in the morning. It looked like they were specially arranging their socks around their legs. Yesterday I saw someone use a file for a shoehorn, and this morning I noticed that every man who took care putting his boots on kept a file tucked into his boot. Jack said it's a superstition. Some people think that if you keep a file in your left boot you won't get rheumatism.

Ten to nine,
Joe

Monday, December 19, 1927

Christmas is coming, the goose is getting fat;
pleased to put a penny in the old man's hat.
If you haven't got a penny, a ha'penny will do;
if you haven't got a ha'penny, then God bless you!

I am in such a Christmassy mood, which started this morning when I realized that this is the last week of school before Christmas break! And my mood was enhanced (Spelling word) at the end of the day when Sister asked Tom to bring his axe to school tomorrow so we can all choose a Christmas tree at dinnertime. We spent this afternoon making decorations.

After school, Alex and I brought lots of the other kids home to the pond and the boys shovelled it off and we all skated (or slid on our boots) until supper. I really hope I get skates for Christmas.

I think I will start reading *A Christmas Carol* tonight.

P.S. I told Will about the Fleet Wing. He insisted on seeing it but when I took him to the loft after skating, it was gone! Mother must have realized that I might have found it during my ramble through the barn on Saturday. I had a hard time convincing Will that I don't know where it is now. Thank you, Mother, for saving my conscience. I hope I don't stumble across the sled again.

I went into Alex and Joe's room to get *A Christmas Carol* off Joe's shelf and I saw his copy of *New Hampshire* by Robert Frost that the Relatives sent him for his thirteenth birthday. I suddenly felt very sad. I miss Pa and Joe so much. The days are busy, but at night when things quiet down, I feel lonely. I miss the whisper of Mother and Pa's voices sliding up the stairs from the kitchen or the parlour, and I miss the sound of Joe and Alex laughing and teasing each other in their room before bed. Well, anyhow, I picked up the book and lay down on Joe's bed and started to read. I got all sobby when I got to "Stopping by Woods on a Snowy Evening" because it is Joe's favourite and it fits this time of year perfectly. The end is my favourite, where he talks about having to travel for miles before he can sleep.

I know I just put in a letter from Joe yesterday, but I miss him so much that I can't keep from reading another one and pasting it in here now. It will be like having him sitting at the end of my bed telling a story.

November 13, 1927

Dear Em,

A priest and a photographer visited camp today. I was glad to see both of them. Some of the men were only excited about the priest, and some were only glad about the photographer, and some didn't care about either. Jack only cared about the priest. He must be a real God-fearing person, because he was first in line

when the father said he'd hear Confessions. After
the Confessions the priest said a full Mass.

Later, the photographer took photographs of the men
who wanted them. I sat for one. Jack did too, even though
he said he hates having his picture taken. He grumbled
while he waited in line and you should have seen him
scowl while the photographer told him how to sit!

It's back to work tomorrow. I'm going to see if I can
get to sleep before the Ten to nine.

Your brother,
Joe

Tuesday, December 20, 1927

We got a Christmas tree for the school today! The Sisters let us eat dinner half an hour early and then we
all went up the hill that leads west out of Mattawa and
found the perfect tree. It was little Anne Lamothe who
found it and everyone agreed that it was just right for
the school. Tom cut it down and brought it in and after
dinner we had regular lessons. The Sisters say we will
decorate it tomorrow afternoon. They keep us waiting
and longing, that is certain. Friday afternoon is to be
the dress rehearsal for the Pageant in the parish hall and
we will present it on Saturday, Christmas Eve.

I always like when events are held in the parish hall
because it reminds me of Pépère and his stories. The
hall used to be Mattawa House, part of the Hudson
Bay Company's old trading post. Pépère used to say,

"You should have *seen* the bales of fur going in and out of that place, by goodness!"

I always liked thinking of bales of fur and how much softer they'd be than bales of hay.

Anyhow, bedtime for me.

Thursday, December 22, 1927

Decorating the tree was fun — we popped corn on the stove and strung it into garlands, and also put up the decorations we made on Monday. I have to go soon, to help Alex find a shepherd costume. For my angel costume, I begged Mother to let me wear my white dress that we bought for Auntie Annabelle and Uncle Mathieu's wedding, but she will not let me. She said that my nice white nightie will be fine. Is my having to wear my nice white nightie in front of the entire town a Duty that I have been given for some misdeed that I've committed? I shall never understand Mother. Besides this, I am to wear the same angel wings that Mary's mother made SEVEN years ago, when Mary's older sister was the angel in the Pageant. Those wings have been used every year since then and despite their being stored in a box in the church hall storage closet, they look as though some boy wore them during a fight. Maybe some boys purposely fought with them on, just to bend them and make me feel miserable.

I realized how ridiculous I was earlier. I will try to be more optimistic. I am glad that I get to be Gabriel in the play, and am thankful that I have something white to wear at all. Last year Angeline Walter was the angel and she wore GREEN because it was the nicest dress she had and her mother didn't approve of her wearing a nightie in public, even for such a religious event.

Friday, December 23, 1927

Uncle Mathieu was waiting for us after school today, to take us to cut a Christmas tree for the parlour. We chose quite a nice one but we're going to wait until Pa and Joe come home to decorate it.

Which just makes me think all the more that Pa and Joe will be home for Christmas soon and the D.S. will be out. Please, please, please let Joe come home first. If Pa comes home first it will be very bad. He will want to know where Joe is and Mother will say she thought he was with Pa, and then .

I will not think about that. I'll distract myself with another letter from Joe. But first, the dress rehearsal went surprisingly smoothly. I hope that isn't bad luck for tomorrow evening.

November 19, 1927

Dear Emily,

    This morning when I woke up, my hair was frozen to the bunkhouse wall! I figure it's because when the bunkhouse cooled off at night, any water that had come out of the wood earlier froze again. My hair must have been touching the wall when it cooled off.

Some of the men get into quite the mischief here. Just like schoolboys. Remember I told you about the sign in the cookhouse that says, NO SWEARING. NO SPITTING? This morning when we went in for breakfast, it said, SWEARING. SPITTING. Someone covered up the NO parts with paper!

Sometimes people play tricks on their friends, too. Before I tell you about this next one, you have to know that in the outhouse here, the women's section of the Eaton's is always the last one used. Well, one day Sam snuck into his friend Matthew's bunk and replaced his Maclean's magazines with that old Eaton's! Then that evening Sam said really loud, "What's this here, Matty, what've you been reading?!!" and he yanked the Eaton's off Matthew's bunk and held it up so everyone could see. Lots of people had a good laugh. But Matthew didn't care. He just wanted to know where Sam hid his Maclean's. I thought he was going to pound Sam, but I guess he figured it wasn't worth having the Push kick him out of camp.

There goes the gut iron!

Love,
Joe

SATURDAY, DECEMBER 24, 1927
Pa came home first. He got here today, just after dinner. It was horrible. Well, of course it wasn't horrible

to see him again, and I was able to savour the first few moments of his arrival. We had finished hugs all round when he asked where Joe was.

Mother just sort of stopped moving and said, "I thought he was up in Témiscaming with you," as if she thought Pa might be joking with her. Pa turned to Mother rather slowly, so that it frightened me a little. I didn't know whether he was very angry or very scared. "Ana, he's been here with you the whole time I've been gone. Right?" Mother's eyes just got more confused and she didn't say anything. "Right, Ana? Answer me!" Pa didn't yell, but his voice was urgent. "N-o-o-o," said Mother slowly. "He left a few days after you and . . . I thought he followed you to Témiscaming! Didn't he follow you to Témiscaming, Daniel? Well didn't he? He's been sending us lett— "

Then I cut in really fast. "Stop!" I yelled. I wanted them to stop worrying and to keep Mother from mentioning letters, but that didn't last long. "He's . . . he's in Temagami," I said.

Then I burst into tears and I told them the whole story. About Joe's letter asking me to keep his secret. I told them *why* he wanted me to keep the secret too, so that they knew we weren't keeping the D.S. simply to see how long we could keep something from them. When I was done my story they sent me and Alex out of the kitchen immediately. No problem for Alex. He had been about to help Mother dry the dinner dishes when Pa came home. He escaped outside. I came up to my room to write this entry.

I can hear the murmur of a discussion going on downstairs — it's been about ten minutes. I don't have the heart or the desire to eavesdrop, but I am probably in trouble.

I think I'll venture down now. It's probably time to start working on supper, and I'd rather face my punishment sooner rather than later. How will I ever remember my lines with all this brewing in my mind? Maybe Joe will get home before it's time to leave and the whole thing will be resolved right away.

I am in trouble.

When I went down to the kitchen Mother berated me the whole time we were cooking supper. She talked about the Fifth Commandment and respect for your parents and learning to make the right decisions. I didn't say a word through it all. My brain was in a flurry, and I was trying not to cry. Mother and Pa are usually so proud of me, and now they think I'm a liar. How was I supposed to know what to do? All I did was what my older brother asked me to. No one ever asked me if I knew anything anyway! Maybe I should have gone to one of the Sisters for advice, or Father Duquette.

This is all Joe's fault!

I have to leave for the Pageant now. Joe isn't home yet.

Sunday, December 25, 1927

It's about four in the morning. Joe is home now but it's not like I hoped it would be. As far as I can tell, nothing is solved. Pa and Joe aren't speaking, and it's as bad as it was the moment Mother and Pa found out that Joe was in Temagami. Except that I'm not in quite so much trouble anymore. I still have to dust the parlour by myself every day for a week, and memorize Sirach 3:2–7, but those things alone really aren't too bad. Joe's arrival home and his explanation of everything helped, and I could tell he was making an effort to help me get off easy. I think hearing his side of it made Mother and Pa realize that keeping or not keeping the D.S. would have been a pretty difficult decision for me to make at the time. Joe even suggested that I show them his first letter to me, to show what he had asked me to do, but they said they didn't need to see it.

And so I am somewhat out of trouble but Joe most certainly is not. Maybe I should relate everything from the beginning so that it will all make sense. And this way I can write about the Pageant too.

We ate supper early, at four, because we had to be at the hall for five, an hour before the Pageant was to start. Alex and Mother and Mary and I packed up all of our costumes and Pa drove us to the hall. The place was in as much disarray as it is acceptable for a church hall to be, with the Sisters herding the children here and there and helping with costumes and calming nervous little ones. Mother and Pa left us there and went to fetch Uncle Mathieu and Auntie Annabelle, Mary went off to help somewhere, and I helped Alex put on his costume. Then I got myself ready. I had a hard time finding the angel wings — Sister Theresa helped me look through the closet but they weren't there. I later found them in their box shoved under a stairwell, along with some rope and a bucket of nails. Anyhow, everything and everyone was finally ready and we waited behind the curtain. I could hear the hall filling up, and once I even heard Pa call a greeting to someone across the room. There was the opening and closing of the doors, and hushed talking came from the crowd. Finally, the Pageant began, and it went almost as smoothly as it could have, with the exception of three things:

1. Mary (also known as Tilly Boulanger) scowled the whole time.
2. Alex's friend Johnny tripped over his shepherd's crook.
3. I *almost* forgot how to start my lines. I think it's thanks to the exposure of the D.S. and me knowing how disappointed Mother and Pa are with me. It felt like I paused forever before I could remember the lines, but Auntie Annabelle insists that she didn't notice my hesitation at all. It's nice to have lovely Auntie A's kindness in the middle of everything.

The Pageant ended, and everyone clapped, and it was after we had taken our bow and dispersed into the crowd to find our parents that I first saw Joe.

And I'm sorry but I must finish this tomorrow, because I am too tired to do it now; I don't want to sleep too late this morning, because despite everything I am still excited about Christmas. I hung my stocking by the fire before coming up to write. I hope I get an orange! And skates.

CHRISTMAS DAY

It's now late afternoon, and I'm here to continue the story from this morning.

I started walking towards where Mother had told us she and Pa and Uncle and Auntie would be sitting but I didn't see any of them. I saw Joe. For a few moments I forgot all about the D.S. dilemma and almost started running towards him, but then I remembered I was at a religious event. I skipped my last few steps and jumped into Joe's arms and he hugged me and we were both laughing. "Thanks, little sister," he muttered into my ear. I almost froze. What did Joe mean by his thanks? Was everything settled between him and Pa? Or was he being sarcastic, thanking me for spoiling his secret?

I guess he figured by my expression that I didn't know what he meant by his thanks because he said, "Really, Em, thank you." I was about to start yelling at him about how mean it was to ask me to lie for him, but then every-one else appeared and we had hugs and congratulations. Auntie and Uncle said it was the best Pageant in years and Uncle told Alex that he looked so natural in his role of shepherd that he should consider making a career of it. Mother told Uncle he was being sacrilegious. Then Alex started right into telling Joe about everything he could think of — the school Christmas tree, the pond, snowball fights — anything.

Pa and Joe didn't stand near each other and they didn't talk. The adults pretended that everything was normal, and I was terribly aware of it. Alex didn't notice anything. Good for him. At least his Christmas won't be ruined by this stupidity.

After I wrote that last sentence I was so angry I got up and threw my pencil at the wall. I had to do *something* and it's too cold to go out and kick the barn.

We all rode home in the sleigh. Mother had brought bricks to heat on the stove in the hall during the Pageant, and for the ride home we wrapped them in blankets and tucked them in by our feet and hands. The ride would have been cozy except for the wind biting and whipping our faces. The cold wind certainly matched the frosty feelings that were floating around between most of the family. The adults still kept pretending nothing was wrong.

Once we arrived home me and Mother and Auntie Annabelle started laying out the breads and cookies and preparing the tea and cocoa, while Uncle Mathieu and Alex settled down in the parlour. Pa and Joe stayed in the barn to unhitch the horses. It was taking longer than usual. I think Mother must have thought that they were reconciling because she sent me out with tea for them.

It sure wasn't a reconciliation.

I was hardly out the door when I heard raised voices. They were near yelling. As I arrived at the barn I kept out of sight. I heard Pa say, " . . . doesn't matter. Especially after what I told you about your Uncle Thomas, you'd think you could have told us." Then Joe, whose voice was considerably louder than Pa's, "Father, I've already *told* you. How many times do I have to say it? Telling someone would have gone against my purpose. I wanted to do this myself. *Myself.*"

Joe must have been mad if he called Pa "Father."

Pa started to say something to Joe about selfishness, but I couldn't stand it any longer so I appeared around the door, trying to look as though I'd been walking the whole way and hadn't stopped just a few steps away. They stopped talking instantly. I cut in right away with, "Mother sent me with some tea for you." Then of my own accord I added hopefully, "We're all about to sit down in the parlour." I held out the tray but Pa thanked me and told me to take it back in and that he and Joe would be in in a moment. I didn't hear any more talking as I went back to the house. They probably finished up in complete silence.

They were in the house not two minutes later. All of us sat in the parlour and the adults kept pretending that nothing was wrong. This time I tried to believe it, and I was fairly successful. Auntie and Uncle were the best at keeping things normal and Alex helped out without realizing it. We all got talking, everyone listening until something one person said reminded another of something that had happened to them and the conversation bounced all around the room like that for hours until Mother announced that it was time to leave again to go to Midnight Mass. Mass ended at three in the morning, and as far as I know everyone but me went straight to bed when we got home. In bed I began to amuse myself with thoughts of what me and Alex and Joe might do today and the next, until Joe has to leave again, but I soon fell asleep.

But I refuse to think of Pa and Joe leaving. Even though their tempers are a little high and they aren't speaking to each other except when it's necessary, I still love them both and don't want them to leave. Right now I will fill my heart with every good thing that has arrived with Pa and Joe.

I have to dust the parlour now. Pa teased us and said that his Christmas Tree Committee approves of the tree we cut with Uncle Mathieu, but Mother says we can't begin to decorate it until the parlour is dusted.

The parlour is clean and I am writing while I wait for the corn to finish popping. I want to write about our

---

I had to leave because Mother called me to the kitchen, using her "Miss Pattersen, you are in some trouble" voice. It turns out that the corn had more than finished popping — it had pushed up the lid of the pot and was spilling out all over the stove and the floor. I wasn't in *too* much trouble, because the corn was for the tree and not to eat. Well, it wasn't *supposed* to be eaten, but it was anyway. What is decorating the tree with popped corn without eating some of the corn?

Anyhow, in the last entry I was about to say that I want to write about our Christmas gifts. I GOT SKATES! They are from Mother and Pa. They purposely bought this pair a little too big so I won't grow out of them so fast. For this winter I'm just sticking rags between the boot and my heel. I haven't had a chance to try them yet but I am determined to soon. Maybe once things have calmed down a little.

Besides that, Alex and I each got a fifty-cent piece, an orange and a package of Juicy Fruit gum in our stockings. I'm saving my fifty-cent piece. We all had a good laugh when Pa asked Alex what he will do with his. "I'm investing it," he said. Mother raised her eyebrows at Pa in an impressed way, and dipped her head slightly in approval. "In what?" asked Joe. "Candy," Alex replied. Mother groaned. "Saint Nick hasn't given you money, Alex," she said. "He's given you a toothache." We all laughed, except for Alex, who didn't see the joke.

This is what I got from Joe: my own copy of *New Hampshire*, that book of poems by Robert Frost. Can you believe it? Auntie Annabelle has said before that siblings can be connected in a special way. I gave Joe a big hug when I thanked him.

Joe's favourite gift is a mouth organ — Mother and Pa paid for most of it, but they let Alex and I contribute a little bit so we could say it's from us too. Mother says we should be thankful that we can afford gifts and that we have such prudent men in our family — many gamble or drink away their earnings as soon as they set foot outside the woods.

No more time to write. I have to spend the rest of the day in the kitchen. Auntie and Uncle are coming over for Christmas supper!

Monday, December 26, 1927

Yesterday's Christmas feast was a delicious success! Auntie's belly is quite large now. I am looking forward to having a little cousin.

Joe and I had a good talk this afternoon. I have calmed down a bit about the D.S. so I was civil when I told him how upset I was that he'd dragged me into it all. He agreed that it wasn't very good of him, and he apologized.

After a bit we got talking about poetry. Joe had come into my room while I was reading Robert Frost. I'd been working on memorizing "Stopping by Woods on a Snowy Evening" and I recited what I knew. Joe helped me through the rest. Then he asked me to read "Keepsake Mill" from *A Child's Garden of Verses*.

> *Over the borders, a sin without pardon,*
> *Breaking the branches and crawling below,*
> *Out through the breach in the wall of the garden,*
> *Down by the banks of the river we go.*

I have that much memorized. My favourite part is, "Dusty and dim are the eyes of the miller . . . " because it makes me think of an old man with faded blue eyes. No one's eyes can be dusty, yet it is easy for me to imagine.

Joe sat at the end of my bed and listened. I don't really like the end of "Keepsake Mill" because the characters are adults then and it makes me a little sad. It reminded me of what Joe has been telling Pa, that he is sixteen and wants to make his own way in the world and that he wants to do it how *he* chooses and not how other people tell him to. I bravely asked him about why he and Pa are still upset with each other. All he told me is that Pa is so stubborn and thinks the whole family should see that what happened to Uncle Thomas is a good enough reason for Joe not to go to the camps.

Then he changed the subject. "What's been happening around here lately? Before I came home, I mean."

I told him about some things that I hadn't said in my letters or that hadn't been mentioned on Christmas Day. I told him about Auntie Mai's visit and how rude the cousins are and about Will and the sled. And how I have been saving his letters to me and pasting them in here whenever I miss him, or whenever things are slow. I begged him to tell me more about Temagami, so he told me about how they make ice roads so it's easier to haul the logs. I've decided to write it down so I'll always have it, since it won't be in any of Joe's letters now.

Once Lake Temagami has a couple of inches of snow on it and it's frozen enough for the men to walk on, they drag poles across the snow on one section of the lake to pack it and make it freeze faster and more solidly. When an area of ice is thick enough, they hook the horses up to an ice harvester and pull it just a little off shore. A hole is cut in the ice with ice saws and they fill the harvester's tank with water, one barrel at a time. Joe sometimes acts as the conductor — he fills the barrel and hoists it up the ladder until it tips over and the water spills into the tank. Then the horses pull the tank over the roads and the men pull out the plugs wherever they want the ice to form.

One tank lasts about a mile, Joe says, and after it runs out they have to go back to the lake to fill it up again. The horses can be hitched to either end of the tank, which is handy because in most places in the bush there is no road wide enough to turn the tank around. So they just hook the horses up to the other end of the tank and head back out to the lake. They usually do this whole thing in the evening, before a cold night — otherwise the roads won't freeze properly. Joe says the frozen roads make hauling a lot easier because the logs just slide along.

Once everything's frozen well, they start hauling logs out of the bush to the lake. Before they do that, someone uses a metal stamp hammer to imprint the ends of the logs with an MC so that other companies will know they're Mr. McMillan's. Most of the logs just sit on the lake, waiting for spring, when they'll be floated down to Mr. McMillan's sawmill in a boom or just on their own.

Joe stopped there and smiled and asked if I was bored. I said no, but that there was so much to remember. "Anyway," I asked, "How do you figure this is going to make you as rich as Mr. Booth the Lumber Baron?" Joe just chuckled and said that the forest was a forest of gold and he was helping to mine it.

I asked him what happens when the gold runs out but he just laughed. "I don't think you have to worry about that," he said, "It would take every man in this country, sawing and chopping away eight days a week, to clear it all out." I guess he's right.

More discouraging news. Pa and Joe had another row today, only this time it happened in the attic.

Mother had taken Alex over to the Princes' because Mrs. Prince offered to give Alex some of Clarence's outgrown clothes and Mother thought it was only polite to bring Alex with her. She had given Pa and Joe the task of carrying the scrap trunk, where she keeps scraps of fabric, from the attic to the parlour. It was while Pa and Joe were in the attic getting the trunk that I heard the row start. And once I heard it start I downright eavesdropped.

I heard Pa say something about Joe injuring himself. Then Joe's voice, in a tone he might use with an excitable horse, said that well, he hasn't been hurt so far, has he? Then Pa's tone got impatient and he said something about the camps not being a game that you played to see how long you could go without getting hurt. Then Pa seemed to realize he was heading in the wrong direction. "Listen, Joe," he said, "let's come to an agreement. Why don't you come back to Témiscaming with me?"

I realized how difficult it must have been for Pa to offer that — it was almost like rewarding Joe for his disobedience. I could hardly believe my ears at Joe's reply: "Absolutely not, Father." Then he started to raise his voice. "I decided to go to Temagami by myself so I could make my *own* way without being MOLLYCODDLED BY YOU!" Then Pa's voice got so quiet I could hardly hear it. "I suggest we get this chest downstairs right now. I have had enough of this discussion."

I snuck to my room at that point, and they got the

trunk to the kitchen with very little noise considering how mad they both were. But then the door slammed twice — once when Joe left, and once when Pa left. I'm glad Mother and Alex were gone. This is miserable.

TUESDAY, DECEMBER 27, 1927

Joe left this morning, early, and without reconciling with Pa. I was a little sad when I woke up and realized that Joe is gone, even though I don't agree with how he's treating Pa. He said that he will try to make it home some weekend soon, but he doesn't know when. If he doesn't get a weekend away, I guess we won't see him again until the middle of March when the season is over — almost three months away. Time will drag by. I wish we could farm in the winter. People like Will and Tilly are so lucky — their fathers need to stay in town to run their businesses.

I have to go say goodbye to Pa. He is leaving now.

THURSDAY, DECEMBER 29, 1927

Will came knocking at the door yesterday and today with his Fleet Wing. I didn't feel like going out, but Mother convinced me. I had fun, I guess. Mother says I have to keep busy to keep my mind off of Pa and Joe. Too bad they were still angry with each other when they left. It doesn't make me look forward to their return, knowing there will probably be another big row.

I finally went skating today! I started feeling pretty gloomy soon after I got back from sliding, but I was tired of thinking about Pa and Joe arguing, so I went out to the pond and spent a good hour skating around by myself. I forgot about everything almost right away, while my mind concentrated on remembering how to skate! It recalled everything pretty quickly and before I knew it I was gliding around easily. It was a nice time.

FRIDAY, DECEMBER 30, 1927

Andrew Roberts is here in the Mattawa hospital, and Pa is home for a day. Andrew broke one of his legs in two places yesterday when the log he was directing to the top of the skidway slipped and fell on him. They brought him to a doctor in Témiscaming, who sent him home today and said it was a miracle he hadn't been paralyzed. They let Pa accompany him, so Pa is home tonight but he leaves again tomorrow.

Pa asked me if I would visit Andrew often. I promised. I was thinking of Joe, and about how thankful I am that he wasn't hurt and about how much it will mean to him if I visit Andrew. Maybe trying to cheer Andrew up will cheer me up too. I am jealous of Will because his brother is home, but I would never want anything bad to happen to Joe or Pa.

It was nice to see Pa acting normally. It's too bad he can't be that way when Joe is around.

I wrote to Joe this evening, telling him about Andrew and how I promised Pa I'd visit Andrew often. I told him not to worry.

Saturday, December 31, 1927

Pa is gone again. Alex and I visited Andrew today. He didn't say much. I think he was in pain, or maybe he was groggy from his medicine. I didn't know what to say to keep him company, so I just hummed a couple songs while I sat.

Today is the last day of 1927!

P.S. I know that *someone* (whose name begins with the letter *M)* is cheered by Andrew's presence in Mattawa. She has been singing all kinds of songs this morning and as I write this I can hear her singing "The Jolly Raftsman O."

Wait . . . she is repeating the last verse!

> *My love is marching through the pine*
> *As brave as Alexander O*
> *And none can I find to please my mind*
> *As well as a jolly raftsman O.*

Poor Mary. I don't know much about beaus, but if they make you sing all the time, I think I'd rather not have any.

Sunday, January 1, 1928
New Year's Day

We went to church as usual this morning and afterwards we went with the Robertses to visit Andrew in the hospital. He was in good spirits and he led us in singing "Auld Lang Syne." Mary came by not long after we arrived, saying that she just wanted to see how Andrew was doing, but she couldn't stay long because she was about to leave to visit her sister in Eau Claire. I feel bad for her. I don't think anyone but me has any inkling that she likes Andrew. Well, as Mother says, God's will be done.

Monday, January 2, 1928

Back to school. The Christmas tree was gone and everything seemed so unexciting. Sister Agatha had no sympathy. We just drudged on doing the same old drudging drudgery.

Saturday, January 7, 1928

BOYS! *Dearest* William came over today and he, Alex and I decided to play hide-and-seek. It was my turn to search for the boys so I closed my eyes and faced a corner of the parlour and counted to one hundred. I didn't find anyone in the parlour so I went into the kitchen to look. No one was there either so I started towards the cellar and Mother called after me to bring up three eggs. I decided to get the eggs first and then go back down to search for the boys. I was getting the eggs and all of a sudden Will jumped out at me and I screamed and dropped two of them back into the crock and THEY BROKE. I almost threw the third at him. "WILLIAM ROBERTS!" I screeched, "YOU ARE THE MOST BEASTLY . . . *PERSON!*" (I couldn't think of an insult that was strong enough that I was allowed to say.) He took a step back.

"I didn't mean for you to drop them!" he said. He sounded like he was telling the truth, but I was a little suspicious. "Well . . . " was all I could think of to say. He stayed to help clean up the mess and he helped Mother and me repeat the entire waterglassing process on that crock of eggs.

Then we went to his house to see his Kodak Brownie. He even let me take a picture. It is of him and Alex acting silly. How realistic.

TUESDAY, JANUARY 10, 1928
Andrew is home now and I went over to the Robertses after school to visit him. I brought my copy of *New Hampshire* and read to him from it. He said he enjoyed it and told me that I'm a good girl. "Joe talks about you and Alex often," he said. "I can see why — Hey, Will, why don't *you* ever entertain your old brother?" Will shot back that if Andrew didn't have broken bones he would've tackled him right there, and we all laughed.

THURSDAY, JANUARY 12, 1928
I walked home by myself today because Will is home sick with influenza and Alex ran ahead to play hockey on the

pond with some of his friends. I said hello to Father Duquette, who had stopped on the bridge and was looking over the railing at the icy Mattawa River, his arms laden with groceries. He said hello and asked me about Pa and Joe and Mother and Alex and how I was doing in school. Fine, fine, everything was going pretty well, I told him. I didn't say anything about Pa and Joe because I didn't feel like bringing that to the front of my mind again.

Father kept looking at the ice. "Do you ever wonder what's going on under there?" he asked. I admitted that I have thought of it before. He smiled. "Well," he said, "I hope to see you take Continuation Classes after Grade Eight, so you can have all of those questions answered." I said I would. Father is so nice.

I mentioned our meeting to Mother, and can you believe what she said? "I hope you were nice and polite, Emily." As though she thought I might have stuck my tongue out at him. "Of course I was," I said.

Honestly, sometimes I feel that Mother has as much faith in me as a lumberjack has in a dull axe.

FRIDAY, JANUARY 13, 1928
Another monotonous day. Will is still sick. I hope it isn't anything serious.

SUNDAY, JANUARY 15, 1928
Will is very sick. We noticed that none of the Robertses were at church today so Mother let me stop over on

the way home. Mrs. Roberts wouldn't let me past the kitchen because she doesn't want me to get the flu too. I pestered her, thinking that it couldn't be that bad, but she wouldn't let me. She told me to wait in the kitchen while she went to tell Will that I had stopped by. Then she came running back down the stairs. "Emily, run out front to the store and call the hospital for a doctor," she said. "Quickly!" I called, but Mrs. Lamothe at the switchboard said that the line was busy. I told her it was an emergency but she sounded impatient and said she couldn't just cut off a call.

So I ran over the bridge to the hospital and told Sister St. Honoré that William Roberts needed a doctor right away. She must have realized it was serious because she didn't say anything, but disappeared from the room and came back not twenty seconds later with Doctor James. He smiled reassuringly at me and said, "Come on, Emily, let's go." We drove back to the Robertses' in the cutter and when we got into the house he told me to wait in the kitchen.

No one was in sight. I stirred a pot of stew that was heating on the stove. I looked out the window. I sat down. Then I heard Mrs. Roberts crying. She came downstairs without the doctor. "Will's delirious," she said. I started to tremble with relief, because I had thought he was dead. "He's talking nonsense, about Andrew and his pa and about sleds and his camera and . . . " She paused and got a faraway look in her eyes. "He had the Spanish Flu when he was five," she said. "I almost lost him." I gave her a hug, with my mind reeling. I never knew that Will had the Spanish Flu. It couldn't be back, could it?

Then I asked where everyone else was, because I hadn't seen or heard Mr. Roberts or Andrew anywhere. "They're up at Klock's Mills, visiting Uncle Alfred," Mrs. Roberts sobbed. Then she went on about letting Andrew make the trip with a broken leg and that she wondered how rough the roads would be. She sagged into a chair and I patted her on the shoulder.

I heard myself tell her that Will was going to be all right. Then I asked if she wanted some stew. Not very tactful. She moaned about the stew and how now she supposed Will wouldn't be having any and then she said, "*What* is that doctor doing?"

We heard him coming down the stairs. "Everything's fine," he said quickly. "He's sleeping now. The influenza came with a fever, as it always does — it's a hunded and five right now. When he wakes up try to give him some food — Ah, stew? Excellent — and wash him with cool water. He's too weak to have a real bath just now."

Then Alex was at the door looking for me and I came home, so I don't know what else Doctor James said. I can hardly believe that it was only a week ago that Will scared me in the cellar. I will pray the entire rosary tonight.

MONDAY, JANUARY 16, 1928

I stopped by Will's on the way to and from school today. I still wasn't allowed to see him, but Mrs. Roberts said he is a little better, although not much. She said that Doctor James told her that all that can be done is to ensure Will gets rest and food. And prayers.

Tuesday, January 17, 1928
Will slept all day.

Wednesday, January 18, 1928
Mrs. Roberts said he ate a good dinner today. I'm still not allowed to see him, so I'm going to write him a note.

Thursday, January 19, 1928
Thank you, thank you, God. Will is getting so much better. He might even be at school on Monday! And I can see him tomorrow on the way home!

Friday, January 20, 1928
I saw Will today. It was a little frightening, because he looked so tired. His eyes were all dark and he stayed lying down the whole time I was there. But he did smile a lot and asked about Alex and Clarence and "old Sis A." I told him off for using such a disrespectful name for our teacher, and a nun, no less. He smiled at this too. I'm still worried, though. What if the fever comes back?

Sunday, January 22, 1928
Will was at church today. He had to sit down a lot during Mass, but he managed it.

Monday, January 23, 1928

Will wasn't at school. Clarence asked if he could carry my books home for me and even though my house is very far out of his way I said yes, without being too embarrassed. We spent the entire walk talking about Will, and we stopped in to see him. It was nice talking with Clarence. I think it made us both feel better to talk about what a good friend Will is.

Tuesday, January 24, 1928

I visited Will again today. He's doing so much better. Mrs. Roberts says he will probably come back to school on Thursday.

Wednesday, January 25, 1928

Today when I left the school, Will was standing at the bottom of the school steps! He had his sled in tow and his skates were slung over one shoulder. "Too ill to come to school, but well enough to skate across the river!" I said. I couldn't help it. "You sound like my mother," he answered.

I grinned, and then everyone was crowded around him, asking him if he had had to take any cod liver oil and if it was true that he had smashed his wash jug in delirium. (It wasn't — I hadn't even heard *that* one.) Throughout all the questions everyone walked up the hill and we went sliding until supper.

Thursday, January 26, 1928
Will was back at school today, just in time for tomorrow's Spelling test. Sister Agatha doesn't seem to have much pity for him. I suppose this is good.

Friday, January 27, 1928
I got a letter from Amelia today. I haven't had one since the summer. I don't know what to think of her. I can't help feeling angry with so many of the things she said. I mentioned this to Mother but she said I should re-member that Amelia is living in a very different place and will be experiencing many more changes than me. Here is the letter.

Saturday, January 14, 1928

My Dear Friend Emily M. Pattersen:

It feels wonderful to be writing to you again after such a long time. Of course, I am always so busy with school, and my friends and I are often in the middle of coordinating some event or another. It was only last week that we all volunteered to help organize the Church's Junior Social. It was something we all agreed to do, so when Lettie Maynard didn't show up for meetings, we didn't speak to her for a while. She is such a flat tire. Well, anyhow, never mind about her. How I wish that you could meet some of my friends! Father says they'll all turn out to be flappers and he hopes to goodness that I won't follow. I think it would be rather fun to be a flapper, don't you? I would love to drive my own car. I don't think I'll ever smoke, though. That may be a bit too rebellious, but as Wilma says, "You never know what might happen, Amelia!"

Well, anyhow, if you were here I'd be sure to take you to the drugstore. It's only a couple of blocks away and they sell the most scrumptious sodas! We stop for one every Friday afternoon after school. John Maybar is always there too, and Jane says that someday he's going to be my beau. Imagine that! I just tell them to be quiet and mind their own business — Oh! I just remembered! We got a car! Father bought it at the end of August. He said that it is the best of the best — it must be, because it has electric windshield wipers! Even Jean's father's car doesn't have electric wipers. Of course the car is put away for the winter. I can't wait for summer so we can take it out again.

How is everyone at your house? Is Alex still annoying? And what is Joseph up to? Are you getting along with Tilly Boulanger? How about those beastly boys William and Clarence and Thomas? I remember they always bothered me so. You seemed not to mind though — funny. I guess it comes from growing up in a house full of boys. Everyone is well here. Annette is studying literature at the university. She loves it and talks about it ceaselessly. Father is always at work and Mother is endlessly involved in everything social, from church bazaars to fundraisers to parades. She thrives upon it.

My birthday is coming up! I am so excited. I just got a bob a month ago and I am sure that Mother is getting me a cloche hat. Annette has one and it is so stylish! I hope

I get some new dresses, too. Except for two new ones at
Christmas, my others are last year's fashions or worse!

Well, I'd better finish this letter now, or the house will
be out of paper! I don't know if I've ever written such
a long letter in my life — I hardly know where I found
the time to write it! I wish I could telephone you, but I
understand that you probably can't afford a telephone.
Besides, it would take too long to place the call anyway.

Sincerely, your Friend,
Amelia A. Forth

P.S. When you sign your name, you should always
include the initials of your middle name. It is more
sophisticated.

I don't appreciate her calling Alex annoying. *I* can
say it because I am his sister — Amelia is NOT. And
about Will and Clarence and Tom! And my house is not
exactly FULL of boys! In fact, I wish there were more in
it — that would mean Pa and Joe are home. And being
dissatisfied with last year's fashions is RIDICULOUS! I
still wear dresses that I wore when I was NINE!

And of course we can AFFORD a telephone! Even
though Pa really wants one, Mother will not hear of having
one in the house because she says that they are unneces-
sary. Why pay for a call and have to wait to be connected,
and then chance being listened in on? Telegrams are much
safer in all respects. She feels the same about electricity.
Miss Adams says Mother doesn't realize what she's missing

by staying with coal oil lamps. Mother argues that if it's too dark to work by coal oil, then it's time to go to bed. I think that she inherited those opinions from Pépère.

And if I were Amelia, I would not be anxious to be a flapper! I think it would be wonderful to drive my own car, but *smoking!* I've heard Mrs. Wilson and Miss Adams talking in town and they say that Mrs. Wilson's daughter-in-law in New York smokes *and* drinks alcohol and that she's got her husband in debt because of it.

I will try to remember what Mother said about Amelia experiencing bigger changes than me. I used to imagine visiting a bigger city than North Bay, but if it would turn me into an Amelia, then never mind.

MONDAY, JANUARY 30, 1928

Another package of letters from Joe today! At least now there is no more fear of Mother picking up the post.

Here is the first one.

January 4, 1928

Dear Em,

You'd probably be glad you weren't here the other night! Even though McMillan doesn't allow alcohol in camp, someone managed to sneak some in and last night they told the tallest tales! The voices got louder and the swearing got worse the later we stayed up. My favourite story was about Joe Montferrand.

Me and you and Alex always knew that Joe M. was a very strong lumberjack and a good fighter for French pride, but Mr. Stevenson told us a story about him that I hadn't heard before.

He said that one time Montferrand and his men went into a bar where the barmaid served them even though she knew Montferrand had no money. So to thank her for serving him anyway, Montferrand kicked his bootmarks into the ceiling of the tavern! Even if it's not true, I like the story. It would be great to live in the old days, when there was so much more glory for the lumberjacks and river drivers. But it's true that the camps were much colder and darker and dirtier and there was more bad blood between the French and Irish jobbers. I guess that now isn't too bad a time to be working in the timber!

Love always,
Joe

THURSDAY, FEBRUARY 2, 1928

Today is Groundhog Day. Mother says it's foolishness but I always like to hear what everyone else says. I don't know where everyone who lives in town finds a ground-hog to look at, though. I certainly don't have all day to wander around our fields looking for one. And what do you do if it's both sunny and cloudy?

I heard contradicting stories about whether we'll have a longer winter. To me, the shorter the better because if it's short, Pa and Joe will come home sooner. Which means the bad feelings will be sorted out sooner too. I hope.

FRIDAY, FEBRUARY 3, 1928

I am sick. It's not much though. Just a bit of a sore throat and a runny nose and a cough.

Also, Mother had a letter from Pa today. It was short, but he did tell us that the men have been feeding scraps to an injured fox that comes by camp once in a while!

WEDNESDAY, FEBRUARY 8, 1928

I got the flu! But not nearly as bad as Will. When I woke up last Saturday I felt terrible and by the evening I was quite sick. It was completely uncomfortable. And Mother told Alex to ask Sister Agatha for my homework so that I could work on it during the day! At least I won't be very behind when I go back tomorrow.

It was a slow, boring time. Will wasn't allowed to visit me in case he caught the flu again.

THURSDAY, FEBRUARY 9, 1928

I'm back at the grindstone, as Pépère used to say. Today was fine, but I was a little tired. Everyone, even Tilly, was nice to me. The girls gave me a get-well note they had all signed.

FRIDAY, FEBRUARY 10, 1928

We stopped on the way home from school today to watch some men hauling ice from the river. The men put the blocks in the icehouse and covered them with sawdust to keep them from melting in the summer. "How big do you suppose the blocks are?" I asked Will. He guessed at about two and a half by three feet. I always feel bad for the horses, having to drag those big blocks up the hill to the icehouse, but then I think of the summer and how wonderful it is to suck on cool chips of ice. Except for having to spit out the odd bit of sawdust.

SATURDAY, FEBRUARY 11, 1928

I had quite a fright this morning! Before dawn, while Mother and Alex were still asleep, I crept into Alex and Joe's room to see if I had left my little Bible on Joe's desk, because I couldn't sleep and wanted to read it. I remembered leaving it there last night. The first thing I saw when I entered the room was Joe's bed, and there was SOMEBODY IN IT! For a moment I wavered between being afraid and running to get Mother, and being brave and facing the villain on my own. I grabbed Alex's hockey stick from the corner and crept up to the bed — and saw that the person was Joe! I was so excited that I wanted to wake him up to say hello, but I knew that I should let him sleep. So I did. I forgot all about the Bible (which *was* on the desk) and went straight to my room and started getting ready for the day. I made my bed, would have washed my face if there had not been a layer of ice on the water in the wash jug, got dressed, went downstairs and lit the fire, fed the pigs and chickens, milked Walter and Bess, and I had just started making breakfast when Joe came down. I ran over to the stairs and gave him a big hug. "How is Joe Montferrand?" I teased.

Joe explained that he managed to get home for a visit, but that it will be his last one until the camp closes in March. I offered to get a bath ready for him but he said that Mother had made him one when he got home last night. He went to the cellar for some potatoes and he peeled them while we talked.

Joe asked about Andrew first. I said that he is healing well and I told him about Will's illness and my flu. I also told him about school and Amelia's letter. He snorted at that.

Eventually everyone was down for breakfast and afterwards Joe came sliding with Alex and me! As we walked to the hill I asked Joe about him and Pa but he just shook his head and said, "He doesn't understand." So I left it.

———————————

The Pattersen residence is to host some very exciting entertainment in a week's time! It was Thomas's idea to have a hockey game and he asked me yesterday if I would ask Mother if it could be on our pond. He said it is the perfect size and there won't be much worry about thin or weak ice like on the river. I asked Mother today when we were all in the parlour after supper and she said yes! I am excited. I don't know yet how they are choosing teams.

Sunday, February 12, 1928
One last day with Joe. He goes back to Temagami this evening. We visited the Robertses after church today because Joe wanted to see Andrew.

Monday, February 13, 1928
Tomorrow is Saint Valentine's Day! I will try to be kind to everyone all day long and I will ask Mother to tell us her Valentine's Day story, even though I've heard it so many times it's one of my favourites. I will save the story for tomorrow to keep with the spirit of the day.

Everyone was talking about the hockey game today. Thomas's sister Sandy, who plays on the Mattawa Ladies' hockey team, agreed to be our referee. Tom said we can pick teams tomorrow so that we will have almost all week to make strategies.

Tuesday, February 14, 1928
I got six valentines today — from Will, Clarence, Alex, Marianne, Sarah and even Tilly! Will's and Clarence's both had the "Roses are Red" poem in it, and so did Alex's, except that instead of "sugar is sweet" he wrote "sisters are sweet."

If Amelia were here we would have spent an hour

making valentines for each other. But she isn't here and she isn't really a friend anymore.

Now for the story of Mother's Most Unromantic Valentine's Day Ever. I'm writing it here so I'll never forget it. I'm sure that if Mother ever has grandchildren they will want to hear it.

It happened early in 1907, when Mother was sixteen and Pa was eighteen, and Pa had just come to Mattawa from England the September before. One day, Mémère sent Mother to the Bell Brothers' grocery to get some coal oil and sugar, and Pa walked in while Mother was waiting for Mr. Bell to serve her. As all love stories go, Pa thought Ma was very pretty, but of course he had no idea who she was or anything about her at all. So after Mother left the store he asked Mr. Bell who the girl was and at Mr. Bell's suspicious smile, Pa pretended to be indifferent. Pa lied that he was just wondering because his sister wanted him to ask her something. But Mr. Bell suspected he knew Pa's real reason for asking. He told Pa that Mother's name was Anastasie, and then he served Pa. Mr. Bell was nice and later offered Pa a job as a clerk at the store. Pa took the job and that's how he got to talk a little with Mother. Mother says she never suspected a thing, and things went on like this until February.

Pa decided to give Mother a valentine on Valentine's Day. He stopped at her house and a very old man answered the door. Pa got so nervous seeing Mother's father that he just asked if he could leave the card for

Anastasie. The man looked at Pa kind of funny but said "sure" and that was it.

Even though he had given her a valentine, Mother never mentioned it to Pa when she saw him. Pa was a little discouraged, but one day he worked up the nerve to ask her if she'd liked the valentine. "What valentine?" said Mother, embarrassed and confused. Now Pa was really embarrassed, because he had embarrassed Mother *and* he didn't know what was going on. "The one I left with your father to give to you on Valentine's Day," he said. Mother insisted that she had never received any valentine. "Well, I left it with your father. I remember he was wearing a faded yellow shirt!" (According to Pa, he could feel his face getting very hot.) It was revealed that Pépère didn't own any faded yellow shirts. And upon further explanation it was revealed that Pa must have gone one house too far — he had delivered the valentine to Mother's neighbour, who also had a daughter named Anastasie. But the wrong Anastasie had worked in Toronto as a nurse for the last twenty years and came home twice a year. Mother laughed and said, "Besides, everyone around here calls me Ana," and that was that.

WEDNESDAY, FEBRUARY 15, 1928

The boys don't want the girls to play in the hockey game! "You'll slow everything down," said Ben, and all the boys agreed, including William. I shot him an evil look. He withered.

"Thomas," I said, turning to him, "your sister plays

on the Mattawa Ladies' champion team! How can you say that none of our group of girls is allowed to play?" "Your *group?*" he laughed. (I will admit that there are only three of us, including me, interested. The others are Marianne and Jeanette.)

"Yes!" I said, taking a step closer. "Our GROUP. And if you won't let us play" — here I couldn't resist poking him in the chest with my finger — "I'll tell your sister!" The boys laughed at this but I turned on my heel and marched off, and (luckily) Marianne and Jeanette followed. It took a LOT of courage, but I walked up to the Wilsons' house and knocked on the door and asked to speak to Sandy. She took our side without hesitation and we WILL be playing on a team on Saturday.

THURSDAY, FEBRUARY 16, 1928
Time to paste in another letter from Joe, I think.

January 12, 1928

Dear Em,

I haven't been bored lately, I can tell you that! I finally saw some cheating at cards. Some of the men were playing cribbage with Sam Lamure and Adam MacDowell. Sam's a log maker, and Adam has the worst job in camp. He's called a chickadee and he travels the camp roads to make sure they're clear of everything from bark to horse manure.

All of a sudden Sam knocked back his chair and yelled, "Say that again, you good-for-nothing chickadee!" Adam stood up and said, just as loud, "I said you're cheating, Lamure!" (I'm leaving out the swear words.)

By now everyone was watching and Mr. Mackey warned Sam and Adam not to let it go too far. Sam said that he had to let it go far when a chickadee told him he was cheating. He shoved Adam backwards and right out the door. Adam got up right away, but quick as a snap, Sam was outside too. There was rumbling inside the bunkhouse while people scraped back chairs to follow Sam and Adam outside. By the time I got out there the fight was already started.

I was sure Sam would win, but Adam moved fast and ducked a lot of Sam's punches. They went round and round until the Push came roaring up, shouting, "EVERY SINGLE ONE OF YOU GET BACK INSIDE THIS SECOND OR YOU'LL BE OUT OF THIS CAMP BEFORE YOU CAN SAY JOE MUFFERAW!" We moved fast, and I was glad I'd been one of the last ones out, because it meant I was closest to the door. Last thing I heard from outside was the Push yelling, "You boys smarten up!" Then he slammed the door and walked off swearing.

Doesn't it remind you of some of Pépère's stories? What a rascal he could be. Do you even remember his stories? We were so young.

Sorry, Sis, Ten to nine. I'll be seeing you soon!

Love,
Joe

Yes, I do remember Pépère Bilodeau's stories, even though I must have been six or younger when he told them to us. He was very young — only ten — when he spent his first winter in a camp in 1870. He'd always chuckle when he told us how mischievous he was — he'd play all kinds of pranks. Sometimes he'd get excited telling us about the spring log drives and log slides and pointer boats. The most exciting stories of all were about the log-jams — how sometimes the logs got caught in the rapids and the men walked out onto them to free them up with peaveys and poles. From what Pa tells us, log-jams still happen sometimes, but not as often as when Pépère was young. Pépère remembered every single one he "unjammed." He said he almost drowned once — he slipped off the log and fell under the water and the currents and timber were working together to push him to the bottom. But somehow he got back up with no more than some bruises. Every time he told that story, he'd end it with, "And a good thing too, or none of youse would be here."

We still have the caulked boots that Pépère wore on the log drives, with the little spikes in the bottom to help him move more easily on the slippery, rolling logs. I think those worn-out old boots are packed away in the attic.

I remember Pépère telling us that when his own father worked in the bush, the timber used to be squared, and the "sticks" were floated all the way down the Ottawa River to Québec City to be loaded onto ships and sent off to England. I asked Pa why they stopped squaring the logs and he said it's because it was wasteful, and there's not nearly as much market for square timber as there is for sawlogs now anyway.

I loved Pépère's stories about the pointer boats too; how they were "the best things invented since the wheel." He said he never felt scared in one, that it was like riding in a sleigh over a fresh field of snow. And it's true. I remember going in a pointer once, in the spring, when Pa worked at the holding boom at the mouth of the Mattawa. I couldn't feel the individual bumps of the waves, and the boat hardly rocked at all. Not like a canoe, where you feel as though the boat will tip and let the river swallow you up at any second.

I miss Pépère.

SATURDAY, FEBRUARY 18, 1928
Today is the hockey game! And we still haven't picked teams. I think the boys are putting it off. They're probably already somewhere in town, scheming. I'd better go see if I can find anyone. We need the teams chosen before tonight. I think I will find Marianne and Jeanette before I look for any of the boys.

Everything is settled. I went out and found Jeanette, but Marianne wasn't allowed to come because she was helping with chores. We looked for Will at the train station but he wasn't there, so we figured he must be with all of the other boys. We found them behind the school. They looked disappointed to see us. They should know that behind the school is not a good hiding spot.

I walked right up to Tom and said, "It's time to pick teams." "Fine," he agreed, "but the captains are boys." I reluctantly agreed to this and they chose Tom and Jason as captains. They began choosing teams and I reminded them that Marianne would also be playing. We girls were chosen last, of course, and the worst thing is that I am on Jason's team and Will is on Tom's. Now there will be hard feelings both ways. At least Alex is on my team, and Jeanette. Marianne is on Tom's.

Will and I aren't speaking. I guess he's glad I'm not on his team because he probably thinks I'll slow them down. I am just fine not speaking to him. Although it was an odd walk home because I was steps behind him all the way to the store and the whole way I felt very tempted to put snow down his back like he's done to me plenty of times. In the end I just glared at his back and hoped that he'd know it.

I was almost too nervous to eat supper but Mother made me. I just wanted to scribble that in here before I get dressed.

WE WON! It was so fun! I skated as fast as I could and I got some goals, even though I was using Joe's hockey stick and it was too tall for me. Sandy was as fair as any referee could be. We won, seven goals to two! It's too bad that

Marianne's team lost. None of the boys are blaming her for it though, and I'm glad they have the sense not to. She played better than some of the boys. Sandy said she should join the Ladies' team in a few years!

Will and I still aren't speaking.

Have to go to bed.

I'm having a bit of trouble sleeping. I don't like that Will and I are on bad terms. Why does he think girls shouldn't play hockey? Does he think that? Or is he just trying to fit in with the other boys?

SUNDAY, FEBRUARY 19, 1928

Will and I are reconciled. Pa would say that after the game our pride got the better of us. I kept sneaking looks at Will today in church, only to find that he was doing the same. It was awkward because we kept looking at each other and then looking away. Then after Mass he walked up to me and shook my hand and said that I played very well last night and that he wished we had been on the same team. "Me too!" I said and everything was fine from there. "Maybe next year," he said, and then Mrs. Roberts invited us over for coffee and cookies. Pa and Joe could take a lesson on reconciliation from me and Will.

I wonder what everyone else will have to say about it at school tomorrow.

MONDAY, FEBRUARY 20, 1928

Sure enough, some boys from the losing team started throwing snowballs at me when we walked into the schoolyard, but I held my head high. I felt like a prisoner who had done nothing wrong but who people hated anyway. "Give it up, boys," said Will. It is nice to know that he isn't ashamed of being my friend.

TUESDAY, FEBRUARY 21, 1928

Mother's birthday is just over a week away. She'll be thirty-seven years old. It's too bad Pa and Joe won't be here to celebrate. But Mother is used to that, I guess. The rest of us are lucky our birthdays aren't during logging season.

Everyone's pride seems to be healing nicely after the hockey game. I am glad I was on the same team as Jason Boulanger because Tilly can't stop sneering at anyone who wasn't and praising anyone who was — except for me. She doesn't quite know what to do with me, because I was on her brother's winning team, but she thinks it's ghastly that girls played — that girls actually *wanted* to play. I can't believe what she said today: "Emily, you made an excellent contribution to my brother's team on Saturday. He says you played well . . . it must come from growing up in a house full of boys." Just like Amelia!

I have a brilliant idea. Tilly should move to Ottawa, right next door to Amelia. They could become best friends and I would be happy.

WEDNESDAY, FEBRUARY 22, 1928
Ash Wednesday

We went to Mass this morning and had only beans and bread for supper. I am hungry now, just before bed, but I'm not complaining.

THURSDAY, FEBRUARY 23, 1928

Mr. Roberts is thinking about buying a *car!* Will told me today on the way to school but he made me promise not to tell anyone because his Pa says that he doesn't want the whole town to "help him make a good decision" and talk about it all the time. He just wants to think it over himself and everyone can say what they think *after* it's over and done with. I wonder if his car will have electric windshield wipers like Amelia's father's does.

FRIDAY, FEBRUARY 24, 1928

I got to talk on the telephone today! It's so exciting and I haven't done it since the summer. I went to the store after school to buy Mother's present. When I got there the phone rang and at first I was excited but it turned out not to be the Robertses' ring — it was three short ones, and the Robertses' is two short and one long. Will had run upstairs to change out of his school clothes so he could go see Mr. Rankin at the train station, and I guessed that Mr. Roberts was in the back.

I was looking at some combs that were on display when the phone rang again. I recognized that it was the

Robertses' ring this time. It rang again and no one came so I ran to the bottom of the stairs as Will yelled down, "Could you answer it, Em? I'll get Pa. He's outside." So I went behind the counter and answered, "Hello, this is Roberts' General Store." It was Mr. Bonfield. He sounded confused so I explained who it was and that Mr. Roberts would be in in a moment. But I guess Mr. Bonfield didn't think it was worth wasting money on waiting so he asked me to tell Mr. Roberts that he had decided to take the ring and would he please set it aside for him. I said I'd deliver the message, and I hung up. Will came in with Mr. Roberts just as I was coming out from behind the counter. I gave him the message and he thanked me and joked that he should hire me as his secretary.

After that I picked out Mother's gift. It is a beautiful comb with a small flower on it. The flower is fake of course, but it still looks nice, and you can't tell from far away. I tried it in my hair and asked Mr. Roberts how it looked. "Very nice," he said. "Maybe you should be our model girl instead!" (Of course I blushed.) I bought the comb and it's very nice, but I couldn't help thinking about some of the other combs on display. One was beautiful and silvery, with stones that looked like diamonds, but weren't. But it was too expensive. I think Mr. Roberts knew that I liked it because he let me try it on even though he knew I couldn't afford to buy it. Sometimes I wonder what it would be like to be rich.

I will think about my telephone conversation instead.

Saturday, February 25, 1928

Today wasn't very exciting, at least not compared to yesterday. Mary couldn't come so I had to help with the breakfast dishes. I wanted to demonstrate that I wasn't happy about this, so I dragged my feet when I walked from the table to the sink and from the sink to the cupboards. Mother told me that I sounded like a Clydesdale and that if I wanted to be one I should ask Whinny and Wilfrid about it. She told me to lift my feet. I did, but she gave me a further Duty anyhow. I had to muck out the barn BY MYSELF, with no help from Alex. I wonder what he was doing while I was out there working. ~~Alex is an annoying, si~~

Never mind. It's not his fault.

Sunday, February 26, 1928

I got my first whiff of spring today. I know that it's nowhere near being spring yet, but I got a whiff of it all the same. It cheers me up. Pa and Joe should be out of the camps in no more than a month, and maybe the bright, fresh land will put them in the mood to reconcile. It always does that for me, even when I'm not in a tiff with anyone!

Tuesday, February 28, 1928

I want to make a cake for Mother's birthday but I can't figure how to make it a surprise.

I have figured it out. I will measure out the dry ingredients here early Thursday morning and drop them off at the Robertses' when we stop by to get Will. I'll ask Mrs. Roberts if I can use her kitchen on Thursday after school. I'll borrow the eggs and milk from her and she can add the cost to our account. I hope Mother and Pa won't mind. I can't say, because I've never kept the cake a surprise before.

Wednesday, February 29, 1928

Everything is planned! Alex bought Mother some peppermints today after school (and ate one on the way home). And Mrs. Roberts said she wouldn't hear of adding the cost of any ingredients to our account. Alex has agreed to tell Mother that I stayed after school to ask Sister Agatha some questions and help her clean the boards. I hope asking your brother to lie to your mother in order to keep something a surprise for her isn't a big sin.

Thursday, March 1, 1928

Today is the day! I hope everything works out.

Everything went wonderfully! Mother didn't suspect a thing! Mr. Roberts was even kind enough to drive me home so I wouldn't have to walk with the cake. I got home just a few minutes before supper and Alex was coming back in from the barn so he opened the door for me and we both yelled "Surprise!" Mother was amazed and she said the cake was excellent. After supper was over and the dishes were done we sat in the parlour and she opened her gifts. She liked them both and she tried the comb in her hair right away! She said she'll wear it the day Pa comes home, if she has enough warning before he gets to the house. And she shared the peppermints with us — one each.

Then she told us the story of how she was born at a quarter past midnight on March 1st, 1891, so because this year is a leap year, her birthday should really have been yesterday, if she were to get precise about it.

Friday, March 2, 1928

Today the Sisters did their monthly choosing of people to go in to school early to make the fire and shovel off the steps in the mornings. For March, Sister Agatha chose Tom to make the fire, and Sister Bridget chose Alex to shovel off the steps. Alex will get 50¢ at the end of the month. He's so proud. He says he wants Pa to help him open a bank account when he comes home. I reminded Alex that having this job means he'll have to get up a little earlier than usual in order to get his home chores done. Nothing seemed to disconcert him. I hope he stays enthusiastic or else he might get in trouble and lose the job.

Saturday, March 3, 1928

I keep thinking about Pa and Joe coming home. I will keep a countdown chart on my desk so I can cross off the days as they pass. Just to be safe, I'll assume that they'll both come home on April 1st, even though it will probably be sooner than that and they won't be coming home together. Including today, they will be home in twenty-nine days or less.

Sunday, March 4, 1928

The Robertses came over after church today. Will brought his Rook game and he, Alex and I played I Doubt It. It was difficult to say whether Mother disapproved or not. I don't see anything wrong with it, as long as no money is involved. There is a bit of lying, but it's harmless. Today was my first time playing and I am going to write the rules in here so I can look them up if Alex and I ever decide to play the game with a regular deck of cards.

First, the entire deck is dealt and the first person places their card face down on the table and says "One" whether they actually placed down a 1 or not. The next person does the same, but says "Two" whether it's a 2 or not. It continues like this all the way up to 14, which is as high as the Rook deck goes. Then it begins again at 1. If you suspect that someone is lying and really putting down a different number, you say "I doubt it" and they show you the card. If you caught them lying, they have to take all of the cards that have been placed down. If you were wrong, then you take the pile. The object is to get rid of all of your cards.

Poor Alex couldn't control himself and either smiled or laughed outright when he lied about his cards, so he lost. I won twice and Will won once. I was lucky the last time because my last card needed to be a 5 but it was really a 14. But I said "Five" and Will didn't say anything because the last time he had said "I doubt it" about my card, I *hadn't* been lying and he had to pick up almost the entire deck.

Twenty-eight days until Pa and Joe come home.

———————————

Alex went to bed at seven because he said he needs his rest before shovelling off the school steps tomorrow. That made Mother and me smile. It was a quarter to seven and he came calmly (which is unusual) into the kitchen where Mother was peeling potatoes and I was looking through the Eaton's. "Mother," he announced seriously, "I'm going to get ready for bed now. I have a long day tomorrow and I don't want to be tired for it."

"All right, Alexander, do what you feel is best," answered Mother. If Joe were here he would certainly have called Alex "Sir John." We heard him walking up the stairs, which was a change from his usual running or galloping up them. Then at precisely five to seven he came back down (NOT on the railing!) in his pyjamas and said, "Goodnight, Mother. Goodnight, Emily. I'm going to bed now because a man needs his rest." Mother pretended to cough. He came over to the table and gave each of us a kiss and hug.

"Did you say your prayers, love?" Mother asked. To

which he replied in a dignified tone, "Of course!" We watched as he headed towards the stairs. We saw him pause at the bottom and then over his shoulder he added, "Night night! Don't let the bedbugs bite!" and he ran up to his room. Mother and I laughed out loud. He's said that every night since he was four and Joe taught it to him. I was wondering if he'd say it tonight because he was acting so regally. I'm glad he said it. That is another story I'll have to remember to tell Joe.

Monday, March 5, 1928

I'm snatching a few moments before school. Alex left half an hour earlier than usual to go about his step-shovelling duties. I hope it goes well for him, and I hope that Tom doesn't burn the school down.

Alex's job went very smoothly, he said. Will and I were talking about the fire-lighting and step-shovelling and chalkboard-washing jobs on our way in this morning and I mentioned offhand that I hoped Tom had remembered to open the flue and wouldn't set the school on fire. To which Will pretended to be amazed. He said he thought I'd have enough sense to realize how much the burning down of the school would benefit the children of Mattawa. I just gave him a Look.

Anyhow, everything went well and the Sisters said that the boys had done a good job in getting the school ready. Alex met me by the girls' side at dinner to tell me all about it. Even though it had hardly snowed last night, he had given the stairs "a good sweeping." And Tom didn't burn the school down, or roast us — not like two years ago when Edward McConnell was in charge of the fire for January. Everyone cooked like turkeys for the first hour of class that month because he always put too much wood in.

TUESDAY, MARCH 6, 1928

I am in such suspense! Today on the way to school Will told me that tomorrow his father is going to put up a sign in the store window that will make me very happy, but he didn't tell me what it's going to say. I pleaded with him all day to tell me, but he wouldn't budge. He only said that if he told me it wouldn't be fair. What is that supposed to mean? He is so stubborn! I think he must love to see me in such suspense — why would he have told me about this sign otherwise? I have to do my homework now, and maybe that will help me keep my mind off of all of this.

Twenty-six days until Pa and Joe get home.

And I will find out what the sign says tomorrow.

WEDNESDAY, MARCH 7, 1928

I found out what the sign said! Mr. Roberts is holding an Artist's Contest! It's in celebration of "The Wonders of Nature" and you can enter any work of art, like a poem or painting or carving. It's divided into two age groups: children ages six to ten, and children ages eleven to fifteen. Each person is allowed only one entry and the entries are to be handed in at the store by Wednesday, March 21. Then Mr. Roberts will send them to Mrs. Roberts' sister, Sarah, who teaches school in a little village down the Ottawa called Petawawa. The judging will be fair, because Miss MacIntosh doesn't know any of us (except Will). Will told me that his Pa got him and Mrs. Roberts to help come up with different themes for the competition. They are: classic, romantic and humorous. There will be winners for each theme. I teased Will that he must have thought of the romantic theme and he took me seriously! He looked at me in disbelief and assured me that his *mother* had and that *he* certainly would never have thought of such a thing.

I think I will try to write a poem — either a classic or a humorous one. I don't know much about how to write a romantic poem. I will begin searching for inspiration.

I forgot to mention the prizes! They are brand new black Watermans! Along with each pen, Mr. Roberts will give the winners a bottle of ink (whichever colour they choose!) and a blotter.

Thursday, March 8, 1928

I didn't hear many people mention the contest today. That is fine, although I suppose not wanting people to enter is being a poor sport.

I set my mind to writing a poem about nature and this is what I have come up with — I have decided to enter the *Classic* category:

The Wind

The wind is magic and a force so wild
It wins the heart of many a child.
For it may play the friend or foe
And will follow the children wherever they go.

A dark storm cloud the winds now blow
To send the children fluffy snow.
And in pretty spring the wind is chill
And blows the blooming daffodil.

The wind is magic and a force so wild
It wins the heart of many a child.
Oh yes! It is loved, and perhaps the best reason
Is that it is there from season to season.

by Emily M. Pattersen
Twelve years old
Theme: Classic

FRIDAY, MARCH 9, 1928

I was just thinking that at most there are twenty-three days until Pa and Joe come home.

What I said yesterday about no one entering the contest changed today. Before lessons began, Tilly was yapping away about it as if she had already won. One of the boys finally called across the room, "What if you don't win?" That seemed to stump her. She was not conceited enough to say that of course she would win, so she just stopped in mid sentence. I can see her still, sitting sideways in her seat, one arm on her desk, the other on the desk behind her, back very straight, her head tilted slightly upwards, and her mouth open (as she had been talking). She closed her mouth and looked down her nose at all of us.

"Well, I don't even *need* a new pen," she said. "I have plenty at home. So if I don't win, I will congratulate the winners."

I must admit that it was a very noble answer. Well, the last part of it was. At least she's not entering the classic category. She's telling everyone she's going to do a *romaaantic* painting.

SATURDAY, MARCH 10, 1928

We received word today that Richard McConnell died in a lumber camp at Témiscaming yesterday. He was a teamster and he lost control of his sleigh — it was going down a steep hill and his load of logs was so big that the horses couldn't keep ahead of it. The men had wanted him to put the Barienger Brake on the sleigh so he could control its speed, but he'd said no, that it would take too much time to hook it all up. The sleigh went off the road and Richard was thrown from the top of the load and crushed under the logs that fell on him.

Uncle Mathieu was the first to hear the news because he and Auntie live by the telegraph station. He came over and told us. Mother cried a little. I think it made her think of Uncle Thomas and Pa and Joe. It made me think of them. And Richard was only eighteen. That is just about Joe and Andrew's age.

His body is supposed to arrive on the train later today. Mother says we'll go to meet it to show Mrs. McConnell that we are here to support her if she needs anything.

Lots of people were waiting on the train platform with Mrs. McConnell. Four of her children were with her. Edward and his father came home on the train too, and it was all very sad. We will pay our respects at the McConnells' this evening. I'm rather jumpy about it — I have been in plenty of parlours for plenty of vigils, but I am not used to them. I suppose that's a good thing. It would be horrid to be used to them. The funeral will take place once the ground thaws out. Alex asked Mother where Richard's body will be until then and she had to tell him about the Dead House behind the church. I think he knew about it before but not in such a serious way.

The visitation was sad. Mother got teary when she saw the white crepe over the McConnells' door (white means someone young has died) and then again when we reached the casket. I'm glad I do not have to go again tomorrow night. Mother will go tomorrow, and she'll bring Mrs. McConnell some preserves and a pie.

SUNDAY, MARCH 11, 1928

Mass was particularly sad today. I prayed extra hard for the souls of Uncle Thomas and Richard, and for the safe return of Pa and Joe. Alex asked me to help him copy out "Cows Eat Grass" because he wants to enter it in the *Humorous* category of the Artist's Contest, but I told him I'm not much in the mood, and he still has ten days anyway.

TUESDAY, MARCH 13, 1928

It's raining! It rained while we were in school, so the snow was very sticky and good for snowballs, which it hasn't been for weeks. There was a superb snowball fight in the yard after school, though I got hit in the face with a snowball that had a chunk of ice in it. My left cheek has a scratch and it's a bit bruised, but it doesn't hurt very much.

The funny thing is that during our snowball fight, Mrs. Boulanger was in the schoolyard to get Tilly, because she was going to take her to Watson's to buy her a new dress (we girls had been made aware of this in the cloakroom days ago) and when she saw me get hit she tsk-ed. "God makes snow fall on the ground for a reason," she said, to no one in particular. "That's where it should stay!"

Clarence (who was on my team) paused to mutter to me, "What about the stuff that falls on roofs and barns and fenceposts?"

The fight didn't stop, but everyone made sure to aim clear of Mrs. Boulanger. Tilly got dramatic and covered her head with her books as she left the yard. I really wanted to aim a snowball at her, but I refrained.

Later we stopped in at the Robertses' for some cocoa and Mrs. Roberts asked me what happened to my cheek. "It's all bruised and scratched, deary," she said. Before I could reply, Will piped up. "She got in an awful fight with Jason Boulanger at dinner. You should see him! He had to go home." Mrs. Roberts put her hand to her chest and looked at me as though I had just dropped in through the ceiling.

Not realizing that Will was joking, Alex said, "No, she didn't, Will. What made you think that? Ben hit her with a snowball after school. Didn't you see?" And Mrs. Roberts released her breath and rolled her eyes and swiped the back of Will's head with her tea towel, but I could tell she didn't mind his teasing. "Well, make sure your Mother cleans it well once you get home, Emily," she said. "You wouldn't want that getting infected." To which Will asked how the cut could be dirty if snow is just frozen water. Mrs. Roberts told him to be quiet and drink his cocoa. And then Andrew popped in (he's finally off his crutches) and said, "What's all this about Joe's little sister fighting the boys?" but he winked at me so I knew he had heard the whole thing and was only teasing.

The rain has stopped. I hope the river doesn't flood like it did when I was six. Some people had to live with friends and relatives for a while and then fix up their houses because the water came right up to their kitchen windows.

WEDNESDAY, MARCH 14, 1928
When I came home my mittens were soaking wet so I put them under the stove to dry. I wish they didn't always dry as hard as rocks. I remember when I was little I used to be afraid of breaking them when I put them on because Joe had warned me that would happen unless I waited until I was outside to bend my fingers. He said there was something in the winter air that kept them from breaking. It wasn't until I was eight that I realized he'd been fooling me!

THURSDAY, MARCH 15, 1928
I have finally helped Alex copy out "Cows Eat Grass" for the Artist's Contest. He's decided to draw a picture of Bess and Walter under his poem.

I am looking forward to tomorrow night, because it will be Friday and that means no school the next day! Mother plans to have Auntie Annabelle and Uncle Mathieu and the Robertses for supper. That's good, because it means games and storytelling and fun.

Friday, March 16, 1928

It is after school but I only have time for a quick note because I'm needed downstairs with Mother and Mary to help prepare the food. Auntie and Uncle and the Robertses accepted Mother's invitation, so everyone will be here and it'll be busy. I just had to write that I did get another letter from Joe. It's most likely the last one of the season so I'll paste it in right away.

It's a sad reminder, for him to talk about Barienger Brakes so soon after we've waked Richard McConnell.

February 18, 1928

Dear Emily:

I hope everyone there is fine. I'm doing well, but I'm beginning to itch to get back to farming!

The latest game here has been to thread miniature model Crazy Wheels. Their real name is Barienger Brake, but most of us call them by their nickname. They say that if you haven't gone insane trying to figure out how to thread the thing, the screech of those turning wheels will do the job!

The Crazy Wheel is really a special brake that makes it safer to drive loaded sleighs down hills. When they want to set one up they string a cable through all of the brake's wheels. Then they attach the brake to a tree at the top of the hill on one end, and to the sleigh on the other. The brakeman at the top of the hill pushes on the Crazy Wheel's lever when he wants to slow down or stop the sleigh. It's a lot safer than letting a loaded sleigh fly down a hill with only horses and a man trying to control them!

We've been hauling like madmen lately, to get all the logs onto the ice before it starts to break up, and before the roads thaw. Jack says we might have to start hot logging soon, where we skip the skidway and haul the logs right to the lake. The ice roads have been keeping pretty well this year. Jack told me to smear molasses on the bottom of my boots and then dip them in the horses' oats to keep from slipping on the ice. Seems to work.

This year, McMillan decided to have some logs built into a couple of small rafts, to have some towed to his mill in a bag boom, and to leave the rest to float down on the spring drive, with men following along. He hires drivers to follow the logs so they can sweep them away from the shores when they get stuck and so they can sort them at the sorting areas and sawmills. Glad I'm not toughing the run like that. I've heard it wears you out, having to get in the freezing water to move along a stubborn log, and then camp out on shore in wet clothes.

So I'm not toughing the run, but I'm staying here longer than some people, which is good because more time here means more money! When I get home I'll have made about $150! It's great to finally be considered a grown-up, at least by the men here. Let's hope that Pa starts thinking that way too.

If there's one thing I want to do before I leave here,

it's build a brag load. It's a challenge for us men — to see how many logs we can pile on one sleigh. It's not meant to be a real load. Mr. Mackey said he remembers one time in 1916 when he worked down south for Big Ed Hoover in Webbwood, and they had a competition to see who could pile the biggest brag load. The men who won managed a load of 306 logs, and they hauled it to the log dump! Jack guesses we might be able to make a load of a little more than 200, if we have time.

I'd better go now. Make sure to wish Mother a Happy Birthday for me on March 1, if you get this letter by then.

Love,
Joe

P.S. Make sure you don't send me any letters after the beginning of March, because I might not get them.

I didn't get the letter by Mother's birthday, obviously. I wonder why this one took so long. Maybe Joe thought he'd have more to add later but never got around to adding it. At least he's coming home soon! Sixteen more days at most.

SATURDAY, MARCH 17, 1928
The feast day of Saint Patrick
I am cozy in bed as I write this — Mary is here today, to cook breakfast and do the dishes. Last night was the

most fun I've had since Christmas. Uncle Mathieu told us a story about a time when he was a boy, one I'd never heard before, so I'll write it down here.

Uncle Matthieu had been out fishing in a creek with Pépère when a lightning storm came up. Pépère knew to take shelter in a storm so he half pulled, half ran with Uncle through the stinging rain away from the creek, over the railway tracks and into an abandoned shed. Uncle swears that the storm was right above them, because the lightning and thunder were happening at the same time and the thunder was so loud that they had to cover their ears. Pépère and Uncle watched the storm from the door of the shed and Uncle saw the most amazing thing. The lightning hit the railway tracks and it made sparks fly waist-high off the rail. Uncle says he has a picture of that as clear as day in his head.

I believe him. I have some pictures like that in my head; pictures that are better than the ones you can take with a camera because they are in colour and really are as clear as day. And they're not blurred or bent or ripped or stained.

Mother told some more stories about her and Uncle Mathieu's antics from when they were younger. One was about the time they got the idea to empty the apple barrel in the cellar and sit inside it and roll each other around! They carefully placed all of the apples in a pile in a corner so that they wouldn't get squashed or bruised. The barrel rolling actually succeeded (and Uncle still declares that it was one of the most fun things he ever did) until Mother got sick from all the rolling and she started crying. Mémère heard her so she went to the cellar and promptly put an end to the barrel rolling. Mother and Uncle both got spanked, and they had to polish all of the apples and put them back in the barrel before they got any supper.

I like thinking of all of the things that happened in this house. But that's it for now because both my stomach and the smells from the kitchen are telling me that it's time to go down for breakfast.

Auntie Annabelle and Uncle Mathieu invited us over for supper this evening to celebrate the feast of Saint Patrick. It was wonderful. Auntie's belly is VERY large now and Mother and me ended up preparing most of the meal. I didn't mind.

Alex found it difficult to keep from staring at Auntie. Mother tried to distract him but Uncle Mathieu noticed and said, "What do you think, Alex? Has your aunt eaten enough to feed an elephant?" Mother and Auntie rolled their eyes and exchanged looks that I couldn't read. "You always were insensitive, Mathieu," Mother teased, slapping his hand as he dipped his finger into a bowl of icing. Alex managed to stop staring.

Auntie let us put our hands on her stomach to feel the baby. Alex said he felt him kick three times. I asked how he knew it was a boy. "Well, of course it's a boy, Em," he said. "I'm going to teach him everything he needs to know, and I wouldn't be able to do that if he was a girl. So he must be a boy." Uncle laughed.

I will be happy whether the baby is a boy or a girl. It will be wonderful to have a new cousin. The adults got to discussing names. Auntie and Uncle agree on Daniel for a boy, but for a girl Auntie favours the name Diana, while Uncle prefers Rose. Honestly, I like the name Rose better than Diana. Diana reminds me of diamonds, which remind me of certain rich people whose names begin with letters like A and T. We will see what happens!

SUNDAY, MARCH 18, 1928

I was bored today but did not tell Mother. I was sitting in the parlour, staring at the painting we have of a winter scene by Mr. Dufoe that Pa bought for Mother for their fifth wedding anniversary. Seeing the painting reminded me of the outdoors, which reminded me of the lumber camps, which reminded me of the box we have in the attic with some of Pépère Bilodeau's things in it. I promptly hopped off of the chair and went to the attic to look through it. There aren't very many things in the box. There is his rosary, as well as his caulked boots with the spikes in the bottom. He told us that he used to show off for the girls on the boom at the mouth of the Mattawa River. He'd hop and jump from log to log, and once, he fell into the river right in front of Mémère! And that was just after they'd started courting, too.

There was also the pocket watch that an Indian gave

Pépère after Pépère saved the man's little boy from drowning. Pépère never knew who the Indian was, but he'd told Pépère he knew the watch to be very old, and he apologized that it didn't still work.

The second-last thing in the box is a photograph of Pépère and some other men squaring a timber. And my favourite thing to look at is Pépère's old Ready Reckoner, the little handbook that some of the men buy that tells them board measurements and everything. They used to be more common. I like it because it has Mémère's handwriting inside the front cover. It is very faded and the corner is torn off, but I know what it says.

À *Ed*

De Anne

Le 1er Octobre, 1883

I wish I had known Mémère.

P.S. Today after Mass, Mrs. Ranger spread the word that the Ladies' Committee will begin discussing a Spring Picnic at their next meeting. That reminded me of summer and church bazaars and other such wonderful things. Everything will seem possible once the snow is gone. Or should I say, everything will seem possible once Pa and Joe are home.

And once the hard feelings between them are cleared up.

Monday, March 19, 1928
My poem must be handed in to Mr. Roberts the day after tomorrow! I'd better write out a good copy now.

Tuesday, March 20, 1928
I asked Will yesterday if he would tell me the results of the contest if he found them out before his pa announces them and he said no! I reminded him about the sled at Christmas but he said this is different because it has to do with his father's business. I suppose he's right, but I want to know.

———————————

Heavens Above! (To use Sister Agatha's favourite saying.) I was beginning my homework and I noticed how close I am to the end of this journal. Maybe I can buy a new one using some of the money I have saved up. I don't want to have to wait until my next birthday to ask for one. Joe calls me a stingy old miser. It is true that I save money from all sorts of things, like Christmas and birthday gifts and sending cream to Renfrew. But I would rather be a stingy old miser with a journal than a flamboyant young flapper without one!

Wednesday, March 21, 1928
It turns out that many more people entered the contest than I had originally thought. I will stop concerning myself about it though, because it will likely be at least

another month before we find out the names of the winners. I would really like to win. I could use a new pen soon, because the tip of mine is wearing out, and this way Mother and Pa wouldn't have to buy one. I was talking about this in the cloakroom today and Jeanette offered me her least favourite pen but I said no thank you. It was nice of her to offer, but it's not up to her to supply me with pens. Besides, she broke in the nib, so I'd likely find it awkward to write with. I suppose that if I don't win the contest I'll have to satisfy myself with a plain old pen from the store.

Thursday, March 22, 1928

DARN! All of this talk about pens seems to have given me bad luck with writing supplies.

My ink bottle broke today, and it was nearly full. It happened because I was barely out the school door when Jason threw a handful of slush at me and I put my hands up to shield my face, and my ink bottle slipped from on top of my books and through my arms. As I said, I was barely out the door, so of course I was standing on the stairs, and when the bottle hit the steps it smashed into a million little pieces. (That is how Alex described it to Mother.) I had to pick up the glass, so I couldn't stop at Will's on the way home because I was late as it was, and I have ink stains all over my hands (and my boots, but the blue on the black is not noticeable), and I feel even worse because Mother gave me money to pay for a new bottle, saying that it's not up to me to buy necessities. I can't wait for the weather to stay warm so that we won't have to carry our ink to and from school. It can just stay in the classroom and won't freeze overnight.

FRIDAY, MARCH 23, 1928

Tilly Boulanger was VERY beastly today. I was almost late for school because I had to buy more ink this morning, and Will couldn't find the ink, so he had to ask his father where it was and then Mr. Roberts couldn't find it, and then he found it behind a box of tobacco. Will had to hurry ahead to get to school on time, so I felt even more late, arriving by myself.

I rushed into the cloakroom at three minutes to nine, and was sitting at my desk at one minute to. That is when T.B. made sure Walter was looking in our direction and said, "Oh! Emily, what happened to your boots? It looks as though you dipped them in ink!" I looked at my boots and didn't see anything of the sort. Like I said, the ink doesn't show unless you hold the boots about two inches from your eye and move them back and forth so that the ink catches the light. I knew that she had seen what happened yesterday and she just wanted to cause trouble.

I looked up, and Jeanette caught my eye and rolled her eyes and frowned, then smiled, giving her head a little shake. I smiled, so Tilly turned towards Jeanette to see what I was smiling at, and then Clarence, who sits behind me, pulled a face while Tilly was looking in Jeanette's direction. The three of us laughed and Tilly turned accusingly towards me. Her face showed that she was coming up with something mean to say, but then Sister called us to silence. It was wonderful, except for the fact that Clarence couldn't stop snickering during prayer, so he got the strap. Poor Clarence. He is so kind and good-humoured, and he makes us all laugh, but the teachers only see him as a naughty child. I wish they

Saturday, March 24, 1928

PA IS HOME! He arrived yesterday evening and that is why I didn't get to finish my entry. I cannot finish it now — I have too many things to tell about his arrival.

It was fairly late when I began writing in here last night, because Mother had decided to dust the parlour after washing the dishes, and me and Alex had to help. When we were finished, we got ready for bed and I began writing. Alex went back down to the kitchen for some milk, and Mother was in the parlour reading.

I was writing when I heard Alex yell, "Mother, go put your comb in your hair! Quick!" It took me a moment to realize what he meant and when everything fell into place in my head I rushed downstairs (and almost collided with Mother, who was rushing upstairs) and yanked open the door to find Pa standing there with his hand reaching out for the knob. I squealed and gave him the biggest hug and then Alex was there too. We stood hugging in the doorway until Mother came back down to the kitchen and told us to be sensible and come inside, for Goodness' sakes — the woodpile was getting low enough without young hooligans letting the heat out. Pa shooed us all inside and closed the door and said, "What about old hooligans?" and he swept Mother up and gave her a kiss. Then he noticed her comb! "Where did you get that, Ana? It's lovely!" Mother said she would explain later, after he washed and put on clean clothes!

By the time Pa was FINALLY allowed back in the kitchen Mother had put on coffee and cocoa and, like at Christmas, we all started talking at once and Pa had to quiet us down and get us to take turns. Mother told Pa about her birthday gifts and the cake, and Pa told us funny stories from the Témiscaming camp.

And would you believe that Mother only let Alex and me stay up for an hour after Pa arrived home? I have never seen the clock's hands move so quickly. After the hour was over we were sent to bed even though it was a Friday night and there is no school today. Mother said that she wouldn't have her children staying up all hours of the night and sleeping until the afternoon.

I vow that I will always remember what it feels like to be a child forced to go to bed on the most festive days, and I will never do the same to my children. It is completely unfair.

I just remembered that I forgot (that is funny if you say it as a sentence by itself) to finish what I was going to say on Friday night. I was talking about how funny Clarence is and I was about to write that I wish that the Sisters would admit that he is funny and not strap him so much.

I am sitting up in bed writing this. I am very tired, but I just want to say that I can hear Mother and Pa talking in low voices downstairs in the parlour. Everything is so wonderful. Almost so wonderful. Everything will be *perfect* once Joe gets home and he and Pa start speaking again. The grandfather clock just told me in his deep, resonating voice that it is nine, so I will put out the lamp.

SUNDAY, MARCH 25, 1928

JOE IS HOME! Unlike Pa, Joe got home in the early evening. I can hardly believe that they arrived home so close together. Now all that remains is for the conflict to be resolved. I sound like a teacher saying that. Maybe I could ask Sister Agatha to come to our house and say it. Then maybe my brother and pa would be ashamed of themselves for carrying on like schoolboys.

What can I do? When me and Joe used to fight, Pa would sit us down and make us tell each other why we were angry. It always seemed that we were fighting for such silly reasons then. Maybe I need to do the same for Pa and Joe. They both have hurt pride. Do they realize it?

Pa and Joe are still avoiding each other. This morning, Pa walked into the kitchen just as Joe was finishing breakfast, and Joe jumped up, almost knocked his chair over, grabbed the rest of his toast and walked outside.

Tuesday, March 27, 1928

I can't believe how long this is dragging on. Pa and Joe still aren't reconciled. Even Alex is beginning to ask them what's wrong.

Wednesday, March 28, 1928

Finally, my family is back to normal!

I woke up earlier than usual this morning, and rather than get up I lay in bed and listened to the early-morning sounds. I heard Mother getting breakfast ready, and I heard Pa go downstairs and talk to Mother. Then Mother came back upstairs to make the bed and tidy up, and I heard the door open and close and I knew that Joe had come in from outside. I crept partway down the stairs to hear if anything was going to be said between him and Pa.

Pa spoke first. He said, "So how about the McConnell boy, eh, son?" He was talking about Richard's death. Then there was something I couldn't hear, and then there was Joe saying, " . . . if I hurt your feelings. I *do* care about what happened to Uncle Thomas, Pa. And I was careful."

I tiptoed back to my room. I didn't feel like hearing about Richard again, and I was sure this was just going to lead to the same argument about Uncle Thomas and about Joe being able to take care of himself. I waited to hear yelling, but none came, although I did hear loud voices for a couple of minutes.

Then I must have fallen back asleep because next

thing Mother was waking me up and she seemed to be in quite a good mood. I asked why she was so happy and she looked at me and said, "It is a mystery to me how men can reconcile by telling stories, half of which are probably exaggerated into falsehood." I smiled. They had done just what I wished they would! When I went down to the kitchen Joe and Pa were both there, drinking coffee. Pa sounded as cheerful as anything when he said good morning and Joe grinned at me and winked.

Time to go! Joe promised Alex and me that he would take us into town and buy each of us a Coca-Cola!

Thursday, March 29, 1928

I am at the end of this journal. Joe was amazed when I told him that. He looked very happy when I said that I had pasted the rest of his letters in here.

I'm glad I get to end on a happy note. Pa and Joe are home, and they are reconciled and that is what makes everything so cheerful. Just a few minutes before I started writing this, I heard Joe say, "I missed seeing the crosses every day!" He was taking about the crosses that the missionaries put on the mountain across the Mattawa a long time ago. I thought about Robert Louis Stevenson's miller and about the Indians and missionaries and voyageurs and lumberjacks and farmers, and that it is thanks to them that I am here. And that reminded me that in less than two months we will be planting the crops and Pa and Joe will be farmers again. I thought of Sunday picnics and warm summer evenings spent with Auntie Annabelle and Uncle Mathieu and the Robertses.

I have to finish now, because I am nearly out of room. But I am only finished for today. Tomorrow, I will be without a Christmas fifty-cent piece, but I won't mind, because I will be busy writing in a new journal!

SATURDAY, APRIL 21, 1928

I'm managing to squeeze in one last entry, because I have news that fits in better with this wonderful old book than it does with my new journal. The first piece of news is that I'm writing this with my brand new Waterman pen — my poem won for my age group in the *Classic* category. And the BEST news is that I have a little baby cousin, Daniel Bilodeau! Alex hasn't let us forget that he's going to show Daniel "everything he needs to know," just like he said he would back on St. Patrick's Day. I wonder if his lessons will include how to slide down the railing!

Acknowledgements

I'd like first to thank my editor, Sandy Bogart Johnston, for helping me with my first book, and for so patiently and good-naturedly walking me through the whole process. Thanks also to Jean Little for being the one to pass along my inquiry. Thanks especially to my grandparents, Lloyd Novack and Lorance (Blanchette) Novack, who truly were my research sources for many of the historical aspects of the lumber camps and Emily's home life.

About the Author

Courtney Maika wrote this novel on her Christmas break, the year she was seventeen. Inspired by books such as *A Prairie as Wide as the Sea* and *Orphan at My Door*, she thought she could weave some of her family's stories about her grandfather and great-grandfathers, who had worked in the logging camps of the Ottawa Valley, into a novel. Courtney decided to write in journal form, as she had been keeping a journal since she was eleven. And she'd been reading all the books in the Dear Canada series. She says, "They really inspired me, so at one point I thought, 'Why wait?'" and she began writing *A Forest of Gold*.

Courtney has published an essay and won several awards for both short stories and poetry. This is her first novel.